Doomsday
and Other Tours
Nine Stories
(Second Edition)

MICHAEL ANDRE-DRIUSSI

ISBN: 1947614045
ISBN-13: 978-1-947614-04-8
****

"Aliens with Candy" originally appeared online at *Perihelion SF*, August 2013.

"Doomsday Tours" originally appeared in *Tomorrow SF No. 19*, February 1996.

"It's a Long Road to the Sky Train" originally appeared online at *Perihelion SF*, January 2015.

"Mad Dogs Raid Mars" originally appeared online at *Perihelion SF*, November 2013.

"Mentally Gifted Mutants" originally appeared in *This Mutant Life No. 2*, May 2010.

"The Ragnarockenroll Overture" originally appeared in the anthology *Air Fish*, 1993.

"The Slushpile Surfer" originally appeared in *Pirate Writings No. 10*, Summer 1996.

"Tex of the Dobermans" originally appeared in *Abberations No. 17*, February 1994.

"White Japan" originally appeared in *Byzantium Volume 2*, 1987.

CONTENTS

MAD DOGS RAID MARS

It was Day 172 of the Overmind Crisis, a revolution started when an emergent A.I. seized control of Mars.

In spite of the upheaval, the Martian beanstalk's capsules were still running in both directions. Inter-planetary business seemed to be booming under the new cyber-theocracy, as capsules laden with goods descended on the two-day trip from orbit to the equatorial station of Mars, while others ascended on the adjoining side. Most of the several dozen capsules riding up the vertical railroad were stuffed with child refugees fleeing from forced conversions, but they were only a tiny fraction of the one million people living in domes along the Mariner River as well as the shores of the Boreal Sea.

On the observation deck in one of the upward-bound capsules, a refugee boy lying among the children crowded on the floor found he couldn't sleep. He fretted about his father, whom he hadn't seen in weeks. He worried about his mother back at the Pavonis Mons station, fervent in hoping that a women's capsule would soon bring her to join him at the orbital station. To take his mind off his troubles he looked up through the clear dome, searching for the next down-bound capsule with a sense that it had been a half-hour since the last one had flashed by.

After a few minutes he spotted the capsule heading toward him on the other track, but it looked so different from all the others he had seen that he gasped in surprise. The cargo hatch at the bottom was open like a flower, and during the brief seconds before the two capsules shot past each other, he saw a number of man-sized objects fall out like seeds. He wasn't sure, but he thought the falling objects were military drop pods, and a tingling wonder of hope and excitement raced through his body, as if he had seen angels swooping down to the strident sound of mili-tary drums.

•

Here we go, thought Grimly Forming inside one of the pods as the side thruster rocket kicked on. The sixty pods angled towards Olympus Mons, two thousand kilometers away to the northwest.

Grim laughed to himself at the strategy. If a warship had approached Mars from Earth, the Overmind would have had weeks to prepare. In contrast, this commando raid was like a lightning bolt coming from a cloudless sky.

Still, he had no experience with drop pods, and the rapid decent caused him a growing anxiety.

At 27 kilometers tall, Olympus Mons was a natural fortress immune to assault from the land below it. Nestled within the extinct volcano's mouth was their target: the fortified temple of the cyber-church.

Grappling with his drop-fear, Grim watched the approaching caldera grow larger on his viewscreen and tried to focus on the action to come after landing. The volcano mouth was 25 kilometers across, rimmed by high cliffs standing kilometers tall that enclosed a floor broken up by smaller cliffs, rough terrain, and the pits of two smaller calderas. The temple complex was on the north side, situated on a plateau between a cliff to the west and a pit to the east.

The mercenary commando mission was to locate and extract the cybernetic node from the temple before the Overmind could react. It was a "smash and grab" job, but the exact location of the device was not known. It might be located on the surface of the plateau, but the presence of tunnel mouths in both the western cliff and the eastern pit suggested that the node could be located in deep tunnels beneath the plateau.

The commandos dropping toward the volcano were accordingly divided into three groups: Cliff, Plat, and Pit. Grim was a heavy infantryman, the sergeant leading the second squad of Plat. Clay, Grim's buddy from a job on Mercury, was corporal for the recon team of the Pit squad.

Closing in on the target, Grim saw how the plateau was not flat but a down-slope from north to south. His job was to drive up that middle, ready to fill in on the Pit side, if needed.

The ground was rushing up. Grim had a brief moment of panic, fearing that something had gone wrong and he was going to pancake. He thought of home back on Earth, the smell of the tropical sea and the bitter taste of exile, but then the pod's descent rocket kicked on, slamming him with g-forces.

Suddenly it stopped and he was landed. The sides of the pod fell away and he jumped off the lander, into the dust cloud raised by his fiery chariot, down onto the orange sands of Mars. Sure enough, it was a lot like Mer-cury, gravity-wise and dust-wise. Looking over a roster of symbols and names in the lower left corner of his viewscreen, he checked his squad of three fire teams, finding that all of the eleven other men had landed without incident. They were soon combat ready.

The mercenaries had achieved surprise. Grim imagined the cyberpriests disconnecting their neural interfaces, groggy in the abrupt transition from techno-nirvana.

First Lieutenant said to move out, and the two Plat squads began jog-bouncing at high speed up the incline toward the scattered buildings of the plateau, any one of which might be hiding the cybernetic node. One fire team from squad one inexplicably went off the cliff to the west, triggering a minor avalanche of red dust. It was highly unprofessional, as their sergeant told them succinctly.

"Mind-control lasers," muttered one of Grim's men.

"Can it," said Grim, halting the spread of superstitious hearsay. It was a given fact that the cyberpriests used their neural plugs to connect with the Overmind, but supposedly the A.I. had become stronger and could even affect plugless people. Mind-reading and subliminal hijacking were a few of the witchy powers it was said to have, but that didn't make sense in light of the reports proving that the Overmind's followers were engaged in forced con-version, surgically installing neural plugs into the unwilling.

A hidden pillbox fifteen kilometers to the northwest opened fire on Plat squad one. Vapor trails of rockets chalked the very thin air, ending with explosions that sent up orange clouds of dust around the leading fire team next to the cliff.

Another strongpoint, this one eleven kilometers to the north, fired a salvo at Grim's team but missed. He ordered his squad to respond, and the men with shaped-charge brilliant rockets in their racks fired them off to converge on the pillbox. The combined attack smashed the strong-point.

Meanwhile the cyber-church militia had boiled up from the ground to come charging down the slope and fire their rockets when in range, still several kilometers away. Grim launched one of the anti-personnel rockets from his rack, exchanging fire with the leading edge. A close explosion knocked him over. He rose up in the swirling dust to do a system check and head count within his immediate fire team.

"Systems?" he asked.

"I lost my canteen and my porn collection," said one mercenary.

Another had lost a few of his ten rack rockets, damaged by shrapnel.

Grim heard over the radio that the Pit squad was fighting militia fire teams sheltered in the two tunnel mouths, and the Cliff group had the same thing going on over at their end to the west. The tunnel openings might be a diversion, or one of the four might be the path to the cy-bernetic node.

First Lieutenant called them forward. Grim relayed the order.

"But sarge, they're charging us!"

He was right. A group was coming straight at them, using long kangaroo jumps. It was a crazy move, nearly suicidal, and a little scary for that reason.

"Hold," ordered Grim. "Ready for close assault."

Using his 10-power magnification, Grim saw that the militiamen had good vacuum armor — not power armor, but certainly more than what the merc recon teams had. He waited until the charging enemy was only one and a half kilometers away, then he ordered his men to fire. Their arm-mounted lasers each blazed forth with burning cyan beams. The militiamen were mowed down in mid-jump, producing a brief rain of body parts and cart-wheeling corpses in the middle range, but there was another militia team coming in right behind them, and a third team bounding in from the northeast.

The fighting was hot and heavy. They wiped out the second team, but the third team broke through . . .

•

Suddenly it was over. The immediate group of invaders was crushed, which caused the victorious novice P2-01 to feel that special surge of elation, the transcending peace said to be a taste of what the Accepted Ones experienced when they merged with the Overmind.

"Yes," said the Adept, reading his mind. "You have all done well."

"Am I accepted now?" asked another novice.

"Once all these invaders have been dealt with, I'm sure you will be."

"Violence is so atavistic," said a third novice. "I feel ashamed."

"It is necessary in dealing with the unenlightened," said the Adept. "They are brutish submen. The Overmind needs your strong arms now. There are few of us who have the muscle memories to work such power armor."

"I am ready to fight again," said P2-01.

"It is good, but first, tell me your intuitions," said the Adept. "P2-01, expand your mind as I have taught you, and read the situation even if you cannot read their minds yet. Is this the entire invading force, or are there others on the way?"

P2-01 felt proud to be given such an opportunity. He looked around, away from the black smoke threading out of the shattered pillbox in the middle distance, the dead novices scattered on the red sand nearby, and toward the beetle-like invaders fighting in their pitched battles against the Holy Defenders.

"There must be lifters," he said. "A few lifters, coming from the west."

"Yes, that is correct," said the Adept, smiling in a way that made the novice feel warm and tingling. "And are the invaders on the ground here all there are?"

"No," said the novice. "There is a fourth group dropping in."

"They blinded our sensors when they started, but we saw no military ship in orbit. How did they get here?"

"From the beanstalk."

"Exactly," said the Adept. "Using civilian cover for their military actions. Barbaric and ruthless. But time is on our side and they cannot win. One day soon you will have your dream and lead a group in the invasion of Earth, but for now you must take your information to the Master. Go!"

P2-01 led the other members of his suicide team in bounding away to the north. There was fighting in the mini caldera on their right, and P2-01 wanted to join in, but they had a mission. As he hurried along his way he thought about the coming invasion of Earth, imagining himself single-handedly going up against hordes of trogs.

Further up on the plateau it was all calm and efficient action. The battle seemed far away, as if it were at the foot of the volcano rather than the top.

They met the Master and P2-01 gave his report, repeating his intuitions about the invaders.

"You have done well," said the Master. "Now you must defend the Holy One! Go destroy the invaders in the pit!"

They happily bounded away then, like the Dogs of War unleashed, and tore into the unenlightened who had landed in the mini caldera. The invaders fell back from them in fear and awe of their righteousness. P2-01's anti-personnel rockets arched over and found their marks with devastating accuracy. The invaders seemed dispirited and confused, operating in such disarray that they could not seem to bring their full firepower to bear.

Fire team by fire team they fell beneath the onslaught, until there was only one lightly armored team holed up in one of the tunnel mouths. A tough nut to crack, but P2-01 was moving in for the kill when an enemy's near miss kicked up a cloud of swirling orange dust, halting them for a system check.

P2-01 could hear the enemy radio chatter as he went through his check sequence. They were worried, scared — perhaps they would retreat in blind panic if he let up on them. But then one voice came through to him and rocked him to his core:

"Grim Lee Forming! This is Clay, Clay Moore, your buddy from Mercury — remember?"

"Clay?" said P2-01.

"Grim, snap out of it! The Overmind is messing with

your head!"

The dust had cleared enough for Grim to see. He had been fighting his fellow mercenaries, so that their dead littered the floor of the pit. With horror he saw that the Killed In Action list in the corner of his viewscreen included many dead by his own hand.

"Clay, my God —" He realized that his "dream" of invading Earth had been taken from his real life, the battles he had fought in Africa before his exile.

"Get it together, Grim! The mission clock is running out — the Ace is coming down."

"They know about the Ace squad," said Grim. "I told them."

"Don't matter," said Clay. "Time for the big push."

"Plat-2, Pit-1," said Grim, "follow me!"

With the berserk fury of the recently deprogrammed, Grim and his team turned around and charged against the defenders on the plateau, using a withering overkill to wipe out the Adept and his team.

First Lieutenant asked Grim if he had located the device during his "scouting" up on the plateau.

"No sir," said Grim, gritting his teeth at the face-saving spin put on his temporary insanity. "It might be in the tunnels. Clay, what about your tunnel?"

"Just a cave, sarge, not a deep tunnel."

First Lieutenant told Grim to take the second tunnel in the pit and report all information for the Ace group that was inbound.

The second tunnel mouth in the pit was to the north. It provided cover for the militiamen shooting out of it, their fire strengthened with supporting fire from militia units on the plateau as well as in the pit. But precious minutes were being lost. Grim ordered concentrated fire, and then he ordered a fire team into the tunnel mouth.

"Report!" he said.

"Deep tunnel, sarge! We're going in."

Close assault was near suicidal, but Grim ordered

another team into the entrance after the first one had gone deeper inside.

"Lieutenant, what's the status on the cliff tunnels?"

"Both just caves. You got something?"

"We're checking the last one now, sir," said Grim. "There's a deep tunnel. I recommend that Plat-2 clear a landing spot for Ace at section 1614, eastern edge of the plateau."

"Do it, sergeant."

Now Grim turned his focus on the plateau, blasting at the militiamen so that the final squad could land without facing close assault. As he fought on the surface, the first team in the tunnel was wiped out in their charge against the militiamen deeper underground, their names appearing on the K.I.A. list in the corner of his viewscreen. Grim held the second team at the tunnel mouth, unwilling to send them further in just yet, and hoping that their pre-sence might lure the militiamen into a suicide charge.

Clay's recon team was the only remnant of Pit-1, now under Grim's command.

"Clay, check out those last buildings," said Grim, talking about the unexamined structures in the center of the plateau. "Just jump in and out."

"Okay, sarge!" said Clay, and his team bounded away, their recon jump-packs moving them along at great speed.

Grim directed his men to concentrate their rockets on another strongpoint to the north. The militia teams on the plateau were sweeping east toward him, but Cliff and Plat-1 were right behind them, setting up for a squeeze play once the strongpoint was knocked out.

"Anders!" said Grim, calling to the team at the tunnel mouth.

"Here, sarge!"

"Report on that deep tunnel."

"Straight in. Several kilometers, at least."

"Give me a number."

"The team made contact with the enemy four klicks in."

"What's the bearing?"

A near miss by the strongpoint sent up a cloud of dust around Grim's team.

"Repeat, Anders — what's the bearing?" said Grim as he went through system check.

"North by northwest."

"Recon report," said Clay. "No node on plateau. Repeat, negative node on plateau."

"Here come the angels," said Grim, noting the imminent arrival of Ace squad. "Hold the perimeter! Keep them back so Ace can land!"

The three fire-teams were coming down in tight formation: two heavy infantry, one combat engineering. Suddenly one team veered off, heading toward the high cliffs of the rim.

"Hey!" shouted Grim. "Pull back!"

The team slammed into the cliff face and was buried in the resulting avalanche.

Meanwhile a militia group had charged past the perimeter to be right underneath one of the remaining drop teams, forcing them into deadly close assault. An-other Ace team was demolished.

The combat engineering team was the only one to survive, but they were vulnerable for a period immediately after landing. Grim rushed his forces in to protect them, and the moment the engineers were ready, he said, "Cor-poral Prase, I've got a job for you."

"Can I dig a big hole?"

"Follow me!"

Grim and his team led the engineers to a spot.

"Right here," said Grim.

"Coming right up." The team rapidly prepared a nucle-ar excavation charge.

"Stand by, Anders," said Grim to his tunnel team leader.

"Ready, sarge."

"Fire in the hole!" said Prase, and then he detonated the

charge.

The resulting crater was impressively deep, but it did not breach a deep tunnel.

The cultists were in a new frenzy.

. . . wave after wave of Australopithecine warriors bearing down on him, fighting for their fictitious homeland in the Rift Valley. Grim held his laser in reserve to use against their human commanders, swinging the gore-splattered cutlass to kill the trogs trying to swarm over his power armor. It was a bad spot, and Grim knew he'd been set up by his own side to take a fall. *Keep moving, keep moving . . .*

Grim snapped back to Mars and found the mercenaries were beating the militia back as he led the engineers to the next spot. He stopped slashing with his arm as if he held a sword.

"Here," said Grim.

"Okay, sergeant . . ."

"Ready, Anders."

"Ready, sarge."

"Fire in the hole!"

Again they failed to find the deep tunnel.

The plateau was a scene from Hell, with rocket trails crisscrossing the sky in every direction, men leaping through the air like demons, and dust clouds mushroom-ing up across the tilted plateau. Reports came in of militia reinforcements arriving in the north.

Even worse, the mission clock had nearly run down. The node would soon link up with the other Martian nodes. The window of time won by achieving complete surprise was closing, nearly closed.

Grim led the group to a third spot.

"Here," he said.

"I can't do this much more —"

"We're running out of time — do it!"

"Okay, sergeant." The engineers went through their preparations for a third time while the heavy infantry fired another salvo from their dwindling supply of rockets into the militiamen within range.

"Stand by, Anders."

"Ready, sarge."

"Fire in the hole!"

"That's it!" shouted Anders. "I can see light."

From above, Grim could see the deep tunnel exposed, and militiamen down there began scurrying around like ants. It was ugly, worse than the trog hordes he had faced in Africa, but Grim was nearly suicidal.

"Ranged fire, into the hole, now!" he shouted, and his fire team poured on the rockets.

"Ready close assault," he said. "Follow me!"

They jumped down the hole, into the maw of the enemy. Lasers blazed up at them and they returned fire.

. . . spraying bullets from his submachine gun at all the soft target civilians below in the crowded shopping mall of home. Women, children, teens crumpled to fold with red flowers blooming on their bodies, white flowers bursting on glass around them. The sharp stink of gunpowder over-riding the scent of tropical sea, Grim saw the nightmare sent to make him recoil, but instead of stopping he went with it, turning it into a personal revenge fantasy . . .

Men screamed and died in the burning cat's-cradle of energy beams, cyan and violet, while others, only grazed, gasped out their final breaths in the near-vacuum.

After the furious firefight, Grim stood in the tunnel, surrounded by dead cultists and a few of his own dead men. To one side, in an unbroken section of the tunnel that came to an abrupt dead end, he saw it.

"Engineers, call a lifter and get down here — we've found the node! Anders, hold the tunnel mouth against re-inforcements."

Grim and his two men along with the engineers strain-ed their powersuit-enhanced muscles to drag the bus-sized cybernetic device until it was under the hole. It didn't look like much, but Grim knew it was the power behind all the weird mind control things that had being going on, from mercenaries running into cliffs to his own team's strange conversion. He wanted to destroy it in superstitious fear, to blot out what it had done to him, but the mission was to take it intact.

The engineers rigged a sling. A lifter appeared, hover-ing over the hole. It was lowering a line when it was shot down. Almost immediately another lifter landed beside the hole and lowered a line.

"Anders, come down the tunnel," said Grim. "Meet up with us at the hole."

The engineers secured the line to the sling. The lifter went up and hovered over the hole. Grim's team and Anders's team stood on top of the node as the lifter began hoisting it up.

"Ready ranged fire," said Grim.

As they came up to the surface again, Grim saw that the recent rout of the militia had given way to a third rally. The fighting was hot and heavy, with the militiamen in a do-or-die frenzy, and the devastated mercenaries still pour-ing on the firepower until the node-lifter was clear.

"Fire at will!" said Grim, and the last of their rockets streaked out to slaughter the enemy.

Then it was over, and they were racing away with the node. The plateau, growing smaller, was pocked with burning strong points and the tiny specks that were dead men. The surviving mercs were piling into the third lifter.

For an instant Grim was happy, but then as the node was entering the cargo bay he felt sick, ready to leap to his death.

"Hang on, Grim!" said a voice.

"Clay? You made it!"

"Just barely."

"That's it for me," said Grim. "I'm not doing this any more."

"I hear that," said Clay. "So what are you gonna do?"

"Head outsystem. Jupiter, maybe."

"Sounds good."

"Hey sarge," said Anders. "Who are you talking to?"

Grim looked around. Clay wasn't with him after all.

He saw it there in the corner, but at first he refused to believe it. Clay's name in the list of those Killed In Action. He hit himself in the side, suddenly afraid that he was still under the spell of the Overmind, seeing things that weren't real.

Drawing a shuddering breath, he said to Anders, "I thought I was . . . talking to you."

THE SLUSHPILE SURFER

Eddy Dwar rolled out of bed at 8:55, grabbed a cup of coffee from the machine in the kitchen, and telecommuted to work in time to beat the rush-hour traffic and log-on to the Acme Publishing House computer before nine o'clock. While his computer navigated its way through Acme's outer security system, Eddy looked out the window to another grim grey winter's day.

"Just think what it must be like in the city," he said to himself as he put on his headset and glove.

He was online.

•

It was virtual noon, and the slushpile surfer was paddling out, watching the horizon for the telltale swell of an incoming set. The place was patterned after San Onofre, California, with nuclear power plant cooling towers on the shore and a certain clean grittiness to the beach. In the water it was a zoo, with the inside crowd a mix of newbies and cools, while the hotshots were out beyond the break-ers, watching and waiting in their usual cliques: the Goths, the Hardcore, the Greens, and the G'Oldies The first two were in the best location, so the slushpile surfer aimed for a spot between them.

Scanning the cliques, he recognized Jargonaut, Captain Jingo, Olivia Drab, and the Esperanto Kommando as the Hardcores (Pink Panzer had apparently left them for the Greens), but there was a newcomer with Astrogoth, Flamin' Pagan, and Baron Volapük of the Goths. This new guy was a long-haired albino with a hook hand.

"Outside."

The slushpile surfer spotted the incoming set of three, and began maneuvering to catch the second one. He caught the wave just as it was about to break, riding down left against the glassy wall, staying ahead of the tube. His board jerked a little, hit by something underwater, and then he nearly collided with Mr. Hook, who was trying to plow through the wave to get to the third one.

"Totally uncool."

A few sets later, there was a really big outsider that everybody was trying to get on. The slushpile surfer caught it at the middle, and glanced back to check the tube in time to see the albino swooping down from the crest, pushing surfers out of his way, dominating the wave.

"Clear the vamp-ramp! Make way for the Hook!"

Down went the Green Witch, back fell Pidgin Man, into the falls went Psibrat.

"Asshole."

•

It was virtual noon, and the slushpile surfer was paddling out, when suddenly a sea otter popped up from the water beside him.

"Number of accesses?" said the otter, his big black eyes peering inquisitively.

The surfer counted the dings and scrapes on his board. "About seven," he said.

"Not so good," said the otter, looking away and rub-bing

his whiskers thoughtfully. "I see our new friend 'Vampire Hook.' *His* board looks pretty beat up . . ."

"Surf bully," said the surfer. He spat.

"Probably true," said the otter. "Well son, it's time to come home." The otter pointed its webbed paw towards the shore, where the surfer could see a parked Woody. The headlights of the Woody flashed once. The otter was gone.

The surfer paddled in, walked up the beach past the shredded remnants of surfboards and surfers (a bikini top with a green theta on the cup caught his eye), and got into the awaiting vehicle. It was a 9600. The interior was a blank, there wasn't even a steering wheel, just a dial that went from zero to 9600 in less than a second. The beach dissolved in a blur of motion and was replaced with a bleak and gloomy house.

The slushpile surfer entered Bleak House. In the antechamber waited a few colorless characters wearing nametags. One read 'Bill Toupee.' Another read 'Ms. Dawn Lode.'

"Catch any fish?" said Ms. Lode.

"Not quite," said the slushpile surfer. "I mean, I surf. I don't fish."

The house spoke. The voice was slow, ponderous. "Only . . . seven . . . accesses? Very . . . disappointing . . ."

"You need something to set you apart from the crowd," said Bill Toupee, in an oily sort of way. "You know, a gimmick or something."

"Well, Astrogoth wears a spacesuit with horns on the helmet," said the surfer. "And the Green Witch has death runes on her bikini. At least, she did. Do you mean something like that?"

"Yeah, that's the ticket. Something with name recognition, label consciousness. Snob appeal "

"It's only for surface," said Ms. Lode. "Nobody really cares about what you're like inside. It's all just for show."

The house spoke again. "Surfer . . . must . . . go . . . naked."

"What?" said the surfer, trying to cover his suddenly exposed crotch. "Hey, this isn't funny, man. Gimme back my baggies!"

"Send . . . surfer . . . out."

"Don't let 'em get away this time," said Ms. Lode.

The surfer was back in the Woody, sans bathing suit but equipped with a new board. The dial went from zero to 9600 and then the slushpile surfer stepped out onto a new beach, shielding himself with his board.

"This isn't funny, man."

The Woody was gone.

The surfer sat on the sand behind his board, refusing to enter the water, until the otter swam up out of the surf.

"Come on," said the otter, standing up on its hind legs. "The water's fine."

"But I'm naked," said the surfer.

"So am I," said the otter. "So what? Who cares?"

"Yeah, well you're just down in the water all the time," said the surfer. "I'm standing up on the damn board where everybody can see me."

"Great gimmick," said the otter. "Come on now, surf's up. Or are you just gonna be a wussy?"

•

It was virtual noon and the naked slushpile surfer was paddling out into a place patterned on Makaha, Hawaii. Slick and glossy. With a grim determination he caught waves and fought to keep ahead of the tube while the board took hits. He noticed now that all the hotshots had something to make them stand out from the crowd: Flamin' Pagan with his external combustion, Olivia Drab with her military hardware, Baron Volapük with his projec-tile vomiting, and so on. The hotshots also seemed to be mainly short-lived, disappearing not long after arriving. Where was the Green Witch, Astrogoth, or Jargonaut? He saw White Light Knight's board literally disintegrate under his feet; the tube swallowed him and he was gone.

The slushpile surfer saw Vampire Hook paddling out, and he knew that the beach wasn't big enough for the both of them. It was high noon.

"Outside."

There was a big set coming in. Everybody paddled into position. The naked surfer caught the new wave along with a dozen or so others. The wave was glassy smooth and phosphorescent, but the ride was strictly rocky-road. The board was taking some serious hits. Buck Naked glanced back for the tube and saw Vampire Hook swooping down, pushing people into the maw, closing in on him fast. And right behind him came the tube.

Buck zigged and he zagged, trying to force Vampire Hook into slowing down. Their boards bumped, and Buck went down to one knee to keep from falling off. Hook's triumph was short-lived: Buck saw the tube close over him, he was too low and too slow to race out of it, and the churning waters took him away.

·

It was virtual noon. The otter popped up in the water beside Buck Naked.

"Number of accesses?"

Buck counted the dings and dents, lingering on the one that looked like a bite. "Twenty," he said.

"Not bad," said the otter. "I guess the gimmick is helping after all. Have you seen Vampire Hook around?"

"I took him out."

"You *what?*" The otter dove down for a while, then came up again. "I don't believe this," it said, baring its teeth.

"He was an asshole," said Buck. "Surf bullies must die."

"You don't seem to have a clear idea of what is going on here," said the otter. "You're supposed to surf, you're supposed to shoot the tube. What is wrong with you? How come you never shoot the tube?"

"I don't want to," said Buck. "Guys get chewed up in there."

"I've had it with you," said the otter, slapping the water. "The next wave that comes along, you better catch it and get tubular, you understand? Or else."

"'Or else' what?" said Buck. "You gonna bite me or something?"

The otter put his forepaws onto the board and leaned forward. "This board is going to disintegrate, then the Woody will come to take you back to the Bleak House, and you will never go surfing again."

This sank in.

"Harsh," said Buck.

"Yep," said otter. "It's do-or-die time. Look sharp, soldier."

•

It was virtual noon as Buck Naked the slushpile surfer slid down the face. The tube was forming behind him. He put his left hand into the wall to help slow down. The tube was closing in. Buck looked to the shore and saw the Woody waiting ominously. The board was dragging some-thing. He looked back to see a great white shark gnawing on the tail. The curtain of water was drawing past Buck, and in his last glance to shore he saw the beach covered with otters at attention. Then the tube closed.

The shark tore him into bits that the smaller fish could eat. Buck Naked entered the food-chain, and ultimately he became food for thousands.

•

Eddy Dewar took a lunch break, surprised it was already noon. He had had a fairly productive day so far, scanning through the slushpile at Acme House, tagging the prospective stories and rejecting the rest. There was one he particularly liked, one about this albino with a vampiric hook-hand. His supervisor, who usually approved most of the stories tagged by Eddy, had already bought a few from today's session via standard contracts and electronic transfers. In a matter of months the stories selected today would appear in the Acme magazine, to be consumed by thousands from coast to coast.

Outside, it began to snow.

MICHAEL ANDRE-DRIUSSI

DOOMSDAY TOURS

"Mind if I join you?" said the middle-aged man with a long braid, startling Guglielm Speer from watching the lights of Campania drifting by below. "I hate to indulge myself alone, even at an hour like this." His braid, worn rakishly down the left side of his chest, looked like a cord of gray silk.

Guglielm waved to the other chair. "Not at all," he said, finding his voice. "Please." The observation deck was otherwise deserted, except for the waiter behind the micro-bar.

"Thanks. The name's Karl Burnham. I'm from Ari-zona, currently in-between jobs, and here on my fourth bitter-moon with a little hussy that'll probably kill me from overexertion before the damn tour's over."

Guglielm half-rose from his chair and bowed as they shook hands. "A pleasure to meet you, Mr. Burnham. I am Guglielm Speer, Pacific Rim liaison officer for Goldstar Sumitomo Band. I live in Shinkyo and I, too, am getting a divorce. My first one."

"Call me Karl. Yeah, there's probably ten divorce parties on board, yours and mine included. As for me, I've done a lot of jobs in my time. For instance I was into RecPharm Distribution before Prohibition was lifted, but now I'm

23

retired and mostly work from home. 'Guglielm,' that's an unusual name. Celtic? Mind if I smoke?"

"Please, go right ahead," said Guglielm. "It's just Italian for 'William,' actually. My parents were Renaissance Fair-ies. You can call me Will or Gil, as you like." The sweetly aromatic smoke began to wreathe the table.

"First divorce, huh?" said Karl. "Well, looks like you picked the right tour — and on the *Hindenburg II,* nonetheless."

"Yes, we're being very traditional."

"How about the worst man, is he really your wife's lover or just a friend playing the part?"

"I'm not sure anymore," said Guglielm, passing a hand over the dark wavy hair of his receding hairline.

"Well, she's not bad looking, but I've seen your hussy and *that* one is a real looker, you lucky dog. She must be great in the sack, am I right?" Karl's pale blue eyes twin-kled from their nests of crow's feet.

"She's just a friend, really, but yes, she is very pretty."

"How about the ceremony? Going to be big?"

"No," said Guglielm. "Just a small thing, a few witnesses. I'll be in white, she'll be in black, very traditional."

"Excuse me, sir," said the waiter as he reached the table. "There is no smoking on board this airship." He looked pointedly at the no-smoking sign and presented an ashtray.

"I don't understand why not," said Karl. "I mean, the cells are full of helium, right? So what does it matter?"

"Company policy, sir. It removes the illusion of danger."

"All right, all right." Karl took in a deep lungful before stubbing the cigarette out. "Christ, in the old days it would've been tobacco, too, another dangerous substance."

"Thank you, sir. Now may I take your order? Some-thing from the bar?"

"Give me a gin and heroin."

"I'll just have another beer," said Guglielm. The waiter

left them, stifling a yawn with the back of his hand.

"So, the Doomsday Tour has become a traditional choice for first divorces, huh?" said Karl. "I guess I understand the reasoning behind it — seeing all these terrible disasters that have happened reinforces the idea that it's nobody's fault, really."

"Yes, 'Shit happens,' as they say."

Karl blinked, then burst out laughing. "You *have* been away from home for a long time, haven't you? I haven't heard that one in ages. You're from America, aren't you?"

"Yes, from Seattle, but I've been in Japan for fifteen years. I guess it shows, huh?" One hand went to the back of his head, then awkwardly came back to the table. The other hand pulled at his long straight nose.

"No, not really," said Karl. "It's kinda nostalgic. But like I was saying, the message of the Doomsday Tour is that nothing is anybody's fault. So your marriage has bro-ken up, so what? Here's Pompeii, here's Chernobyl, terrible accidents just happen."

"Makes sense," said Guglielm. The drinks arrived, and Guglielm insisted on paying.

"Okay, but I'll get the next round. Now we went on Doomsday for the first one, and that suited me fine. The marriage was for love, I guess, a breeding contract, but it must've been just lust, if you know what I mean, since I got sick of the kids almost as soon as they were born. Too late for re-negotiation." He scratched meditatively at one of his long white sideburns. "The next one was for tax and legal benefits, with a no-kid clause, and for the end we went on the White Man's Burden in Africa, where the message was something like 'one party is always exploiting the other party,' so a bad marriage is a master-and-slave relationship. Trouble with that idea is, now you're assign-ing blame and both partners may have very different ideas about who is the master and who is the slave. But then on the third bitter-moon we went on the Atrocity Exhibition of Europe. Jeez, all those Nazi death camps and whatnot really drive home the message that there is evil with a capital E in the world, which tends to make the soon-to-be ex-spouses more nasty than usual. So for the fourth one, I thought 'To hell with that, go with something you know that's halfway pleasant,' and came back for a second Doomsday Tour. Of course, we were in motor coaches most of the time on the first Doomsday, different hotel every night."

"That must have been hard," said Guglielm.

"You get used to it, but this zeppelin is much better that way, like a floating hotel. We all like it since we don't have to pack and unpack all the time, and the company likes it 'cause they get a cut of the hotel industry. But enough about me, how long have you been married and which of the many roads brought you to divorce?"

"About eight years," said Guglielm. "And kids, basic-ally. She wants to have them, I don't."

"Marriage contract?"

"It's pretty standard. Without a no-kid clause, which in hindsight was pretty stupid of me, I guess."

"At least you've got the sense to get out before she has them," said Karl. "I sure wish I'd 'a done that, would've saved a fortune. So what was it that got you, anyway? Love, lust, or convenience?"

"Convenience, definitely. My *boss's* convenience. After the earthquake, you know, the anti-foreigner feelings were running pretty high. Every single white male in Japan was seen as a defiler of native women. So my boss matched me up with a single white female employee of lower rank."

"Wow! No kidding? That's so . . . *medieval.* Was there a lot of pressure? Would you have lost your job if you said no?"

"There was a lot of pressure, but I'm not sure if I would've lost the job or not. Anne, my wife, probably would have gotten fired. Women still had it pretty rough before the Chinese came."

"What a story," said Karl. "But what I said about the message of this tour is doubly true for you — *it's not your fault.* How perfect, a perfect fit for you."

•

As soon as they arrived at Pompeii, tour director Christina turned the group over to the local Camorra representative and vanished. The summer day was hot and dry as they walked up to the ancient gate of Porta Marina, where the flagstones seemed ready to sizzle.

"Over here, you canna see the ruins of-a da Temple of-a Venus," said their local guide. "Sadly, it wuzza already destroyed by the eartha-quake ina sixty-two A.D., so we don' really know what-a she looked like."

He led them into the neighboring ruins of the Basilica and told them something of its history. A few European couples on vacation tried to attach themselves to the group, but the guide spotted them immediately and told them off, his hand resting with casual menace on his hol-stered pistol. The foiled freeloaders drifted away.

At the Temple of Apollo the group made a beeline for the small drink stand, while the guide shouted over their heads that one free drink was part of the package and that the orange juice was for the curious.

"Well, I'm curious," Guglielm thought to himself. He picked up one of the paper cups instead of the bottled sodas, but hesitated when he saw the frothy red fluid within it.

"Blood oranges," said someone beside him. "Taste a little closer to grapefruit." Guglielm drank the pulpy mixture and found that it was true. The tour resumed.

"This-a temple wuzza built in-a da turd century B.C. and there were several differen' gods an-a goddesses worshipped here, like-a Apollo right here, and Diana over there on the other side. Mercury was also probably here."

Guglielm found himself at the front of the crowd near a bronze statue that he took to be of Apollo. One of the statue's feet was shiny from people touching it like pil-grims.

"Hey, donna toucha da statue, eh?" snapped the guide, but it was too late, Guglielm had touched the shining foot and jerked back as if shocked.

"Oh, *sumimasen,*" said Guglielm, bowing and rubbing the back of his head with his hand in embarrassment. "Sorry." There was a strange taste in his mouth, the adre-nal tang of surprise mixed with the blood orange juice into a metallic taste, making him think of bronze. The guide gave him a strange look before leading the group to the next location.

The ruins seemed to shimmer in the heat, their terra-cotta colors rendered vibrant, minute details of texture visible from a distance. A crowd of Chinese tourists went by, and Guglielm shed his English, laughing at their jokes and trying to tell them how close Mandarin was to Latin, with each word carrying its own grammar, even though he'd never had Latin but that was what the teacher had said on one of his first Chinese lessons. They looked at him askance, then they were gone, and a breeze kicked up the archaeological dust and volcanic ash, swirling it around.

The ancient city seemed to come to life for him. The busy market stalls, the cramped shops filled with goods, the greasy smoke from the fast food restaurants, the narrow streets with their stones rutted by chariot wheels, all seemed to throb with a life force that transcended time. There was a thundering sound like a hundred chariots driving through the city, and Guglielm laughed out loud, looking around at the others, but he saw solemn faces with tears in their eyes. The thunder came again and many began openly crying. His wife Anne was sobbing un-controllably, with his brother Iago holding her, trying to comfort her despite his own tears. Guglielm's hussy was there beside him like a forgotten shadow, with him and yet apart, as sad and alone as a fledgling fallen from the nest.

"Hey," he said. "*Kimi,* what's this? What's the matter?" He took Julia in his arms and laughed, turning her away from the crowd and towards the ruins. "Look, silly girl. It's alive. Alive." But she only burst into tears.

He tried to comfort her, talking softly, sitting her down onto a bench, and stroking her dark pageboy hair. After a few minutes she began kissing him passionately, tears still running down her face. Guglielm looked back toward the group to find that most had drifted away, that Anne and Iago were gone. For the first time, the thought of them together made him angry, and as his mood blackened, Julia led him by the hand down a narrow alleyway to a small cubicle with flowers above the door.

"Guglielm, please," said Julia. "I need you."

"No."

"Why not? Please, I'm begging you." Her dark eyes seemed all pupil.

"Julia, we're just friends, remember? We've been through this before."

"What's the matter with you?"

"I don't know. I feel funny," he said. "Everybody's acting so strange, and I'm mad at Iago for taking away Anne." Julia had taken off her pants and panties. Her petite size, the cut of her hair, and the oversized white shirt made her look almost boyish.

"It's the juice, and the jealousy," she said, her breath hot against his neck. "Bitter-moons are all about jealousy. Do it to me, Guil. Do it to me to get back at her."

So he took her in rage, lifting her up and pinning her against the wall in an ancient prostitute's cubby.

•

Afterwards he added shame to his mixture of dark thoughts. "What about the juice?" he said. "It was drugged, wasn't it?"

"Of course it was, dummy," she said, pulling her pants back on. "Why else did we get so sad, or think that the volcano was erupting when they did that thunder-thing? It's almost worn off now, but that was really great, just like being there at the end of the world."

They walked around in the ruins by themselves, not talking, until their beepers went off, calling them back to the *Hindenburg II* and the tour. . . .

To Salerno, where 521 people suffocated on March 2, 1945, when a train stalled in a tunnel. . . .

To Avezzano, east of Rome, where thirty thousand died in the earthquake of 1915. . . .

To Sevesso, just north of Milan. . . .

"Welcome to Sevesso, toxic ghost town," said Christina, her voice muffled by the paper filter mask. "Disaster came here in July of 1976, when a vat of trichlorophenol at that chemical plant over there accidentally overheated and burst, releasing an enormous cloud of chemicals which spread over the town. There were around 17,000 people living here at that time.

"At first the incident seemed to be just a minor inconvenience, since trichlorophenol, which was used for surgical soap, isn't really dangerous, even though it is irritating to the skin. However, it turned out that overheated TCP changes into dioxin, one of the most poisonous chemicals, and pretty soon people became sick. Livestock, pets, and wildlife simply died in their tracks. Large areas of the town were evacuated, barricaded, and guarded by soldiers to keep people out of the danger zone we are standing in right now. Nearly 2,000 people required continuing medi-cal attention and around 50,000 animals within the danger zone were slaughtered and disposed of to keep them from spreading the poison.

"But after all this they discovered that there was no way to decontaminate the town. Dioxin is not water soluble, so rain has no effect on it, and no ordinary fire is hot enough to destroy it. In fact, burning the buildings would only put the poison back into the air again. So the inhabitants were permanently relocated, and this danger zone stands as a testament to human folly and the capricious nature of disaster.

"Now then, in order to reduce your chances of exposure, we shan't be here for more than an hour. Remember to keep your decontamination suits on at all times, and yes, that means no trysting in the ruins. Also, absolutely no souvenirs."

"Anne, can I talk to you?" said Guglielm. "Alone?" Iago glared at him, but Anne guardedly said okay.

They walked together into the twentieth-century ruins. Music was blaring from speakers at the perimeter, "Love will keep us together. . . ."

"Ah!" he said in surprise. "Music from before we were born."

"It's period music," she said. "Music that was playing on that day, doomsday."

"Oh, yeah," he said. "Well, we're pretty far into the first week, how do you like the tour so far?"

She laughed, her eyes mocking over the veil of her filter mask. "Oh, it's been amusing. And very interesting at times. But look, you didn't call me aside just to talk about the weather. What's your point?"

"I, ah, I don't think this is a good idea," said Guglielm. "I guess I'm having second thoughts."

"You *guess?* You always guess, Guil, that's one of your character flaws. Now what is it you're guessing about this time? The tour?"

"No, the divorce."

"Oh, that," she said, suddenly interested in the nearby architecture. "Well, it's a little late, don't you think? Or should I say, don't you guess?"

"Come on, Anne. Give me a break. Look, we had *omiai,* an arranged marriage, but that doesn't mean that I don't care for you, maybe more than I thought before."

"*Maybe?* Guil, you're hopeless. Laughing like an idiot at Pompeii, and now practically kneeling on poisoned ground to try and make up. Listen, Mister Lovelorn, we still have our little problem, don't we?"

"How can you be so insistent about having kids?" said Guglielm. "Look around you, Anne. Take a good look. *This* is the world, an ugly, contaminated wasteland. How could you even consider bringing life into this hell?"

"Save the Gnostic Zen for yourself," said Anne, the steel now in her voice, the fire in her green eyes. "This is no more the world than a theme park or a rock garden is. After the divorce you can become a goddamn monk for all I care, in fact, you probably should. But as for me, I want children and I'm going to have them, with or without you."

Guglielm caught himself absently fingering the medallion through his shirt. Its image rose to his mind's eye: the stone lion Hero of many names biting the tail-biting Serpent of matter and reincarnation, causing the Demiurge to release the tail, thus breaking the cycle. And the second-level mantra of the Hero's names was already on his lips. "GA-JO-MO-MI-AH . . . GA-JO-MO-MI-AH. . . ." Gautama, Joshua, Mohammed, Mithra, and Apollon.

Anne spun on her heel and began stalking away, turn-ing only to say, "It's a good thing Iago doesn't have the same soul sickness that you have!"

And the tour went on. . . .

Alongside the Valais Alps, where the avalanches of the "Winter of Terror" killed two hundred and sixty-five in 1950–51. . . .

To Venice, where the fire of 1106 caused a great deal of damage. . . .

"What a lame excuse for a disaster," said Karl Burnham. "They're just trying to attract another tourist circuit, on top of the history and honeymoon crowd they've already got. Look, they haven't even finished the damn sky dome, for crissake! It was just the same when I came here ten years ago."

"Then there's the 'damn dam,'" said Guglielm.

"Yeah, right. And tomorrow we're going to see one of the marvels of Italian dams, to help put it all into per-spective."

•

Guglielm and his hussy Julia walked the streets of Venice, instantly recognized as tourists since the local people all wore Renaissance clothing as a point of civic pride. Many of the Doomsday tourists flocked to the street vendors selling period-style trinkets and accessories: decorative silk hairnets, colorful codpieces, linen skullcaps, frilly garters, and baroque jewelry.

"It sure beats Milan," said Julia as they drifted on. "I can only take so much of the 1950s era, even if it's Italian Motor Industrial."

"Maybe you mean, *especially* if it's Italian Motor Industrial?" They laughed, and she held his arm. "This is wonderful. My folks would've loved it. I was born in Venice, you know."

"Really?"

"Well, Venice, California," he admitted. She groaned and punched him in the arm. "We moved when I was really small."

"And now you've returned from abroad," she said, sweeping her arm up towards the skyline and the unfinished dome beyond. "The city is yours."

He laughed.

"You're happier now than before," she said.

"Before when?"

"Oh, about a week ago."

"Yes, I guess I am," he said. "No, I am. I don't know what it is. Did they slip us some more drugs? Or is this place really magic?"

"Maybe they just spray something in the air all the time," she said, and they laughed.

"It is very easy for me to pretend that we're in love, walking along these narrow, mazy streets, crossing plazas, crossing bridges on our honeymoon," he said. She stiffened slightly, then relaxed again.

"Guglielm, I'd help you if I could. But a divorce is a divorce; it's bitter and vicious no matter how much we mask it. If you can think of a way, I'd be glad to help you get back together with Anne, but it might be that jealousy is the best lever, if not the best revenge."

"He who hath a Will, hath a Way," said Guglielm.

"If it's any consolation, Iago hasn't been spending that much bedtime with Anne lately," said Julia, and the tour went on. . . .

To Vaiont Dam, where 2,000 people perished as whole villages were swept away in the 1963 flood.

To Zagreb for the 1974 train wreck (153 killed) and the 1976 airliner crash (176 dead). . . .

It was past Midnight. Guglielm lay on the lower bunk of the cabin he shared with Julia, but his dark and boyish hussy was sleeping somewhere else again. Guglielm thought of watching TV, perhaps renting a movie from the ship's computer, but the library seemed stale to him after the first week or two of shipboard life, and overstocked with porn. He lacked the energy to do anything but lie in the dark. He tried to will himself to sleep with the hum of engines as a lullaby, but sleep didn't come. The memory of the poker game kept coming back to him, how that fifty-something Michael Casey had been boasting about all the sex he'd been getting from all the 'luscious' thirty-some-thing women, even Anne who 'danced like a mink.' The whole thing made Guglielm sick, the predatory pyramid of fifty-somethings preying upon thirty-somethings, and thirty-somethings like himself preying upon twenty-some-things like Julia; passengers preying upon crew, crew prey-ing upon passengers; one big incestuous dysfunctional family ecosystem.

And yet, behind his disgust there was an even greater longing for Anne. Paradoxically, she was not sullied by the depraved actions of others; she was somehow ennobled.

Guglielm concentrated on the engines again, then filtered out the hum and heard the random creaking of the ship. He felt that he was the skin of a drum, every movement in the area causing him to vibrate, or that his nerves stretched out through the ship like a spider's web, with him at the center.

A woman's laughter in the distance brought him crashing back to his bunk. He was alone and lonely. He was jealous of his brother and all the others who had trysted with Anne, but to his own confusion he felt a passion for her like he had never felt before.

If I could tryst with her, he wondered, *would the divorce be called off? It might be, I don't know the grounds. Should I creep into her bunk wearing only a domino, or insist by gestures that the lights remain out until after the deed had been done? Like a thief in a harem. This is all Iago's fault. He was the one who planted the seeds of divorce. He doesn't even love Anne; he's only doing all of this to make me miserable, just like he always has.*

A new sound began, the sound of slapping skin and moaning from the cabin next door. It was too much. Guglielm threw on some clothes and left.

•

"We have to stop meeting like this," said Karl Burnham, sitting at Guglielm's table in the observation car. "People will talk. *Garçon,* bring us two beers, *per piacere.* Hey, three languages in one sentence, I'm a real European now."

"What was that joke about the EEC?" said Guglielm. "They wanted a society where the cooks would all be like French chefs, the police like British bobbies, the lovers like Italian lovers, the bureaucrats like the Swiss, and the engineers like German engineers. But they ended up with a hodgepodge where the engineers seem French, the bureaucrats act like Italians, the cooks serve British cuisine, the police are like Germans, and the lovers seem Swiss."

"Yeah, that's right. And their military was supposed to be like the old NATO but turned out to be like . . . well, like Antioch, two years ago now. Hey, remember that cocky little Mafioso back at Pompeii, our guide? He said to me that the three big mafia armies are going to get togeth-er to liberate Turkey, just like the Americans liberated Italy during

World War Two. I had to laugh, but I'm telling you, the guy was serious, and said that they were hoping that the U.S. would back them up once the shooting started. Good luck to 'em, I say, but hell no, the U.S. is not coming back to Europe, come hell or high water."

"Speaking of Pompeii," said Guglielm after taking a swig of beer, "I was really surprised by the stuff in the orange juice, and I've been meaning to ask you about those drugs."

"Ooo, 'drugs,' what a hint of evil," said Karl, laughing. "You kill me, kid. It's like you just fell off the Moon or something. Now look, that stuff for the curious is just RecPharm. It's all part of the New Tourism thing, where they tailor a mood or a sequence of moods for a set location and then have the machines mix up a batch."

"Huh. Well, at Pompeii, I was laughing while every-body else was crying —"

"You were? So that's who that maniac was!"

"And then, when everybody was getting all soft and sexy, I was getting very angry."

"No kidding?" said Karl. "I've never heard of such a thing, but it sure sounds like an abnormal reaction. Maybe you just got a funny cupful, or maybe it's your body chemistry."

"Good evening, gentlemen," said Christina, entering the observation deck. "Or should I say, good morning?"

"Ah, Christina, the tireless tour director," said Karl. "I was surprised you didn't mention anything about the Yugoslavian break-up during our tour of Zagreb."

"Wrong tour, that would be on the Atrocity Exhibition," she said, laughing. "But even then we couldn't do it. Seriously, they're still a bit touchy about all that. Maybe in a few more years. . . ."

And the tour went on. . . .

To Oswiecim in Poland (because it was along the way) where four million prisoners were exterminated at a death camp named Birkenau. . . .

To Krakow, where a great fire in 1850 destroyed large

parts of the city. . . .

To Chernobyl.

Even after all the other disaster sites, Guglielm was impressed by Chernobyl. The town was really and utterly deserted, unlike the many towns that had recovered from their setback, preserving the doom as a museum, or Sevesso, where people still lived in the area beyond the danger zone. It was like being on the surface of the Moon, an illusion furthered by the decontamination suits and bulky gas masks the tourists had to wear. The reactor sar-cophagus was a monumental edifice of timeless antiquity, steel and concrete like some kind of modernist cathedral of asymmetrical brutalism, cracked and broken like the weathered remains of an alien pyramid at the bottom of the ocean.

A local member of the *nomenklatura* was introduced as their guide. His heavier lead-lined suit and helmet made him look like a deep-sea diver.

"And remember, no trysting, stay on the path at all times, do not remove your suits for any reason, and abso-lutely no souvenirs," said Christina. "Never forget, this place is hot-hot-hot! If you get lost or separated from the group, do not wander around. Stand still and press the panic button on your beeper. Okay? All right, have fun and I'll see you in about an hour."

A few old and battered Geiger counters were handed out to group members who volunteered to help and the tour began, taking them around the town, surveying the silent death, spiraling inexorably inward towards the sarco-phagus. Then they entered the radioactive sanctuary and threaded a careful path through the labyrinth, a strange cross between bland Soviet industrial architecture and the bizarre mineral formations seen in the deepest caves. The names for the different stations of the sarcophagus were whimsical and eerie, similar to those given to cave forma-tions. Here was a modern ancient power, a new Stone-henge.

When they emerged from the monument, a quick head

count revealed that two were missing. Christina radioed the Ukrainian guide, saying that two panic buttons had gone off. The Ukrainian cursed up a storm and stamped his feet like a bear before going back into the sarcophagus.

"And God damn it, the rest of you stay put!"

The missing couple turned out to be Karl's wife and Iago, the rear guard who had managed to get lost themselves. The tourists were herded through decontamination, where they were allowed to keep their film dosimeter badges as souvenirs.

The *Hindenburg II* turned south, stopping at Kiev for a brief tour of the vast civil defense fallout shelter network beneath the city, "wisely built for a disaster which never materialized," and then a night out on the capital.

At Odessa, two days later, Karl Burnham collapsed on the Potemkin Stairs during the chemo-historical recreation of the 1905 riot and massacre. Guglielm, rendered more terrified than riotous by the cherry juice curiosity, went to help Karl, thinking that his friend was only acting out his role as a victim of Czarist forces. He was surprised to find Karl unconscious.

"Must've fainted," said Karl when he came to a moment later and found Guglielm shielding him from being trampled.

"Yeah, you okay? Maybe you should stay down for a while."

"I still haven't recovered from all that fun in Kiev," said Karl, standing up shakily. "Ah, I'm getting old. I should avoid the curiosity for a while. Funny, I'm sober now. Is it over? Did I miss anything?"

"I'm sober, too. I guess that was the end. Hey, I thought you were just getting carried away with the whole thing."

"Huh. Maybe I was. What a finale, huh?"

"Yeah, just like the movie," said Guglielm. "Do you want to see a doctor or something? You were out cold, you know."

"Nah, it's no big deal. I'll see the ship's doctor later.

Don't worry, I'm not *that* old."

•

A few days later they were at Poientari Citadel, the castle of Vlad the Impaler just north of Curtea de Arges in the Transylvanian Alps of Rumania. The small fortress had been turned into a museum of both fifteenth century military horror and twentieth century cinematic horror.

"This is the *real* thing," said their local guide with great pride. "Do not be fooled by places to the south, like Bran Castle, claiming to be 'Dracula's Castle.'"

"Hardly a disaster site," Karl had muttered. "Just another atrocity, like Odessa and Auschwitz. Advertising for your next tour."

They drank their cranberry juice curiosities, Karl abstaining, and went on a tour of the castle, seeing a lot of very realistic models of human heads mounted on pikes, writhing bodies impaled on poles, and a torture chamber filled with horrific devices collected from around the world and across the centuries. The drinkers, with one exception, seemed possessed by fear and dread; Julia's eyes were dilated and she clung to Guglielm's arm with an icy grip. In contrast, Guglielm felt very much alive, conscious of the blood coursing through his veins, perhaps even slightly courageous and eager. Not for the largely legendary horrors, but for the martial side of the historical Vlad: the pageantry, the chivalry, and the clash of arms.

The guide seemed to be talking directly to him when he turned to lecture the group at the bottom of a staircase. "I know that it may be considered wrong of me to talk to you for a moment about recent events, especially in your current state, but just as you now feel fright, if only for a moment, so are we here in Europe living in constant dread of the New Caliphate. Antioch would not have been such a failure if other nations had joined the British and the French, and if America had come, Turkey would today be undivided. So please don't forget us, and as you see these horrors of the past, consider those yet to come in the future."

As he mounted the stairs, Guglielm fancied himself Vlad the Conqueror, fighter of Turks, returned to his castle again for a brief stay in-between battles, or risen from the dead to save Transylvania in its hour of need. He heard a pained gasp behind him and turned to see Karl, pale-faced and clutching at his chest, vomiting blood, then falling over to tumble down the stairs. Guglielm rushed down, past Karl's screaming hussy, wondering if Karl had somehow been shot.

•

The official cause of Karl Burnham's death was fatal injuries sustained in the fall down the stairs. It was decided that Dominique, the widow, would stay with the tour to Istanbul, the next stop on the itinerary. Christina would find an airplane flight out for Dominique to accompany her husband's body back to the States.

Passengers and crew were deeply saddened by the death, and all of the social events were canceled for the thirty-hour flight to Istanbul. Even the computer games in the diminutive casino were switched off.

Guglielm went to the ship's sickbay to pay his last respects to Karl. As he entered the room, Dominique was pulling a black matchbook from Karl's breast pocket, and she gasped suddenly as if she were about to begin crying, so Guglielm quickly turned and left her to be alone with her husband.

•

Guglielm dreamed of his divorce ceremony.

He stood dressed in white before the judge and to his left was Julia in red, who showed him a large ring on her finger. "Look," she said. "A poison-ring. I got it in Ven-ice."

To his right was Anne in black, with her veil drawn back until the moment of separation, and beyond her was Iago, grinning in green. The ring-breaker stepped forward, the device in his hands, and Karl, who was the judge, said, "Now I don't want you two to start bickering over the pieces. Whatever falls on your side of the aisle is what you get." But as the process began, Karl started coughing up blood, and Guglielm woke up.

•

Istanbul was on the tour as the portal for the Black Death in 1334, but its current refugee crisis made historical disasters seem distant. All of which made the need for "touro-dollars" that much more acute.

"With a history as long as ours, of course there are plenty of disasters," said their local guide at the beginning of their bus tour. "The problem is in selecting the few out of the many."

They spent most of the day at it, from the plunder of Byzantium by Galatians in the third century B.C. through the fall of Constantinople in the fifteenth century, the slum clearance programs of the twentieth century, and the present refugee flood of the twenty-first century. Leander's Tower was noted for the shipwreck near it in 1979 that took fifty-one lives and unleashed a minor ecological disas-ter in the southern Bosphorus.

Christina and Dominique joined the group at dinner in their hotel in the Sultanahmet district of the Old City. "The airport was an absolute madhouse," said Christina. "We spent all day there and couldn't get a simple flight to the States until I finally threw a bloody fit. Now she's all set for an afternoon flight tomorrow."

The hotel room's large bed was a welcome change from the airship's bunk, and Guglielm fell asleep as soon as his head hit the pillow. In the next instant he was answering the phone with dawn peeking at the window and somebody pounding on the door.

"Hello?" he croaked.

"This is your wake-up call," said the voice. "Please have your bags ready and meet your tour director in the lobby in ten minutes."

"What?" said Guglielm, but the line had been disconnected. He put on some pants and answered the door.

"Come on, Guil," said Anne. "The city's under attack. Get your stuff together and hurry downstairs. Where's Julia?"

"I don't know."

"She'll turn up. I'll see you downstairs, okay? I've got to tell the others."

•

"All right, listen up," said Christina in the lobby ten minutes later. "Quiet! Please. Right, well, this throws a real spanner in the works. We've got to get out of this area immediately. The airport is under attack, but Captain Yves managed to get the *Hindenburg* away from the aerodrome. We've decided that the best way for us to get onboard is for them to pick us up from the nearest place. Now, it's a bit unorthodox, but we're going to board the airship from the roof of the Old Market in the Covered Bazaar. . . ."

It was a short and hurried walk to the Covered Bazaar, punctuated by rumbling explosions in the distance that sometimes sounded distressingly close. The gate to the Bazaar was locked.

"Shit," said Christina. "They won't open 'til eight! What time's it now, five? Why didn't I think of that?"

"Are there any other gates?" said Guglielm.

"Yeah, several. Could you run around that way to the next one, find out if it's open? Someone else, please go the other way. The rest of us will stay here, together."

Guglielm jogged off to the left. The next gate was also

locked, but he could see a lot of people inside the Bazaar and heard the tinkle of breaking glass.

He went back to report. After a few more minutes, Michael Casey returned from his scouting mission, telling them of a gate smashed open by a car. The group hurried to that gate and gained entrance to the Covered Bazaar, a dimly lit labyrinth of sixty-odd streets and four-thousand shops, many of which were in the process of being looted.

"No, no, Mr. Mead. Please! This is not a simulation — we don't have time for looting. Stay with the group."

After a number of false turns, the narrow tunnels gave way to a cavernous room, where one brave shop owner, seeing fifty people making a beeline towards him, prepared to shoot them. Christina called to him in Turkish, explaining their quest.

"I'll help you," said the Turk. "Let me come with you."

A few minutes later found the tour group, augmented by the shopkeeper and his family, amongst the domes on the roof of the Old Market. From this vantage point they could see military hovercraft zipping across the Bosphorus to the east, and their airship hanging low above the city to the north.

"Hello, *Hindenburg*," said Christina into her phone. "We're here, come and get us."

"My God," said Guglielm to those around him. "Look at the size of it. You lose perspective from living on it and landing at open fields."

Nearly eight hundred feet long, the airship seemed to be hugging the ground at an altitude of three hundred feet, dwarfing the entire mosque complex of Suleiman the Magnificent as it passed by. The floating giant seemed capable of snapping off the nearby towering minarets with only a gentle bump. It came closer and lower, until finally it blocked out the sky, hovering twenty feet above the group.

A rope ladder was unfurled and the passengers scrambled up. Once everybody was onboard, the engines revved up, the ballast tanks released a load of water, and the airship began turning towards the northwest in a steep climb.

Guglielm followed the crowd into the portside dining salon, everybody laughing and chatting with nervous relief, watching out the windows at the chaos on the Sea of Marmara. Christina was shouting something about moving to the other salon, Iago was hugging Dominique, and Guglielm was making his way aft towards Anne when there was a bright flashing roar that left the aft bulkhead open to the sky.

Screaming people tumbled out, sliding down the steep deck as klaxons blared. The room was rocking violently. Guglielm found himself anchored beneath a table bolted to the floor, perfect form for riding out a Pac Rim earth-quake. Further forward, people were already forming human chains between such posts and the walls, but near the rift Anne clung by herself on the last round table, while Dominique and Iago held onto the wall table.

Like a spider Guglielm made his way over to Anne across the rolling deck, helped her up and over to the web of survivors. There was another explosion further up in the zeppelin, which shook Dominique free of her perch. She slid to the edge before catching herself, her legs kick-ing air. Iago wasn't moving, so Guglielm set out again, crawling down the port wall this time, using the window frames as anchor points.

Iago was blackened and bleeding. Guglielm crawled past him, got a good grip on the last whole window frame and extended his lower body towards Dominique.

"Grab my legs!"

Dominique seized his ankle with a talon-like grip and began climbing up his body, her long white hair whipping in the wind, her yellow gloves making her clumsy. Guglielm lowered his left hand to help her. She took it and seemed to tug. He looked down at her in surprise, seeing that she was now braced against the wall.

"Help me, Iago!" she called, tugging again. He tried to let go of her hand and return both hands to the sill, but she held him in a fierce grip and suddenly he felt another's hands descend upon his lone anchor.

Guglielm began to panic, knowing that he was about to be murdered, and realized in an absurd flash of insight that it was not a black matchbook he'd seen Dominique take out of Karl's breast pocket, it was the film dosimeter he'd gotten as a souvenir of Chernobyl, the blackness indicating a deadly dosage of radiation. He tightened his grips with both hands, pulling her towards him. She yanked him free of the wall, but lost her purchase. Someone else gripped his right hand as Dominique's glove slipped off into Gugli-elm's fist, revealing a strange pattern of burns on her hand for an instant before she fell out of the airship.

Looking up, Guglielm saw that his savior was Iago, backed up by a chain of others.

•

The airship broke into two sections that drifted apart, blown by the wind towards the Bosphorus, descending rapidly but not in free-fall. The city at war drifted by underneath them, soldiers and looters, policemen and refugees, oblivious to the fragmented airship except for the occasional pot shot. The crew passed out life jackets and as the water came closer everybody braced for the impact. A few people cried out just before the ship hit the water to the north of Leander's Tower, but the crash landing, while hard, was by no means lethal.

After the landing, the crew herded the passengers through a side gangway and up a long curved ladder to the top gangway.

From here it was a short climb to the upper obser-vation platform normally off-limits to passengers, and Guglielm went there with several others to watch the invasion as they drifted down the Bosphorus. Everyone was in a state of shock and exhaustion.

Michael Casey walked up to Christina. "Chris," he said,

"you've done the best you could, but I've just gotta tell you, this tour is a total disaster."

•

Iago was sitting on the outer skin of the zeppelin, apart from the others, with his chin resting on his knees. Guglielm approached quietly and sat down beside him.

"Thanks," said Guglielm after a few moments of silence.

"What for?" said Iago.

"For, uh, saving my life."

"Oh, yeah. Glad I was there. Wish I could've saved Dominique, too. Just out of reach."

Guglielm held back his surprise and tried another approach.

"So you liked her, a lot? I mean, I didn't know."

"Yes, I did," said Iago.

"Did you, uh, *love* her?"

"I think so. It must sound funny, I mean, I never thought that I would ever be attracted to an older woman, but she was so beautiful and sexy . . . now she's gone. And what do I have to show for it? There's this, look, a handkerchief she gave me as a present, and that's all I have left of her."

Guglielm was quiet, looking at the handkerchief.

"Hey," said Iago. "Don't feel like it's your fault. You tried to save her, but she just fell."

"So what happened with you two at Chernobyl? Did you tryst?"

"Yeah. She blindfolded me by turning my headgear around. It was pretty intense."

"Well, Chris is worried that you're sitting too close to the edge here," said Guglielm. "If the ship starts to roll you might fall off. Come back to the safe area."

"I will, in a minute."

•

"How's he doing?" asked Ann when Guglielm return-ed to the platform.

"He's in shock, but he'll be okay."

"It was a pretty shocking experience."

"What did you see?" said Guglielm. "How did it look from where you were?"

"What, do you mean about Dominique? She was trying to climb up, but then she stood too fast, lost her balance."

"She lost control, started jerking at me."

"That's right, she did," said Anne. "She must've gotten hysterical, I know I nearly did." She held her arms against a momentary chill. "We're all in a state of shock. We must be. What a nightmare. Look, here comes Iago, back to the fold. God, he looks awful. I must look pretty bad, too."

"No, you're beautiful." He hugged her.

"Guil, darling, I don't want to ruin the moment, but you know that nothing has changed between us." She pushed him back. "Same old problem. Thank you for sav-ing me, but the divorce is still on."

"No," said Guglielm. "We have no problem. I've changed."

"What?" She looked into his eyes.

"I give up. I capitulate. I want to have kids."

"You're in shock." She looked away. "You don't know what you're saying."

"I'm in love," he drew her closer. "I've woken from a long slumber."

"What about your religion? Tomorrow or the next day you will go back to it."

"I renounce it. All the suffering we've seen in these doomsdays has challenged whatever belief I had. It occur-red to me that to be a true believer I would have to commit suicide to reject this world, but I've never really wanted to kill myself, so why dally with this cult?"

"I never understood why you took it up in the first place," said Anne. "It was right after your parents died. . ."

"Well, not *right* after, but that was a part of it. Maybe it was too easy in our tidy world of Japan, but now, seeing a blade of grass pushing up through the pavement makes me think that life can't be all evil. The prisoners in the death camp didn't quit fighting to live, so why should I?"

"I don't know. I'd like to believe you, but it will take some time."

"Okay, watch this." He fished up the medallion from beneath his shirt and tugged it, breaking the clasp. Then he climbed up out of the observation platform and marched over to the spot recently vacated by Iago. In the distance he could see a Red Cross delta-dirigible coming towards them. Guglielm looked down at the medallion in his palm, spat onto its image of lion and snake, and threw it as hard as he could over the edge. It twinkled in its arc, then dis-appeared, and Guglielm began waving to the Red Cross delta.

TEX OF THE DOBERMANS

Yosemite City, July 28th 2102
Revered Dominatrix Wanda,

The weather here continues to be favorable, and work on Half Dome monument is proceeding at a brisk pace. Already it bears the unmistakable features of our Glorious Queen Victoriana, and I believe that it will be completed by the end of autumn, at which point it will be a marvel to rival those of the ancients.

Enclosed herein please find the document you requested, the last written record of our field agent Edgar Burroughs. We at the museum cannot help but feel that young Burroughs was the victim of foul play. His sense of duty was impeccable, his piety exemplary. In the eight years of his service, he zealously sought out ancient writings in the Motherland and Her Colonies, always on the lookout for heresy and transgression of the Law.

In addition to fulfilling his archeological duties, Burroughs always set down in writing whatever odd bits of oral tradition that he came upon in his travels. The docu-ment which follows is of this kind. It was found by porters at Mercy Station, and since Flagellatrix Stella left the train at Bakersfield it stands to reason that whatever fate befell

Burroughs came between those two points. As you undoubtedly know, he is mute, and would be unable to cry out if set upon by persons with evil intent.

I earnestly pray that the mystery of young Burroughs's disappearance will soon be solved. As for the recent find in Her Majesty's Colony of St. Bernard, I trust that the Church will soon give us a verdict.

Goddess Save the Queen,

Thomas Atkins,

Curator

•

The tale you are about to read is currently in circulation among the commonfolk in the southwestern area of County Saint Bernard, near the Wastelands of Ross. Like many tales, there is a factual thread to it: in this case, an unresolved local mystery surrounding the disappearance of a gentleman scientist, and the destruction of his mansion by fire.

My work for the Queen's Museum of Antiquities often takes me far afield, but I must admit this was the first time I had ever visited the quaint and charming community of C___ in the district of Lake A___. After a bone-jarring coach ride, it is a gift of the Goddess to encounter the hospitality of a good inn, a tasty supper, and an early bed. Such is what I found at "Angel's Roost," an inn near the town wall, owned and operated by a Mr. Angel Clare.

One evening after supper, towards the end of my stay, an itinerant storyteller entered the common room of the inn. He was a perfect picture of the type, being gaunt of body, scraggly of beard, and imbued with the dust of the wildlands. Despite the latter, his turban and flowered waistcoat were rather clean. As this character of fable approached the bar for the customary pint of ale ('to prime the pump,' as they say), I detected an instant of hesitation, as if a galvanic current had passed between the storyteller and Theresa, the barkeep (whom I had not seen before that evening, but later I discovered she was the pro-prietor's wife). Perhaps I imagined it, for the moment passed without incident: greetings were exchanged, the coin was offered and refused, and the storyteller took his pint to sit at a table, nodding to the two constables at the table nearest my own, touching his forehead at the sight of the lieutenant of the Queen's Amazons sitting with them. He did not seem at all surprised to see an Amazon, even one who was not wearing her top hat and veil.

The constables traded pleasantries with the storyteller, who gave his name as Norman Bean, and learned that he had recently come from the Wastes, that he had never before visited the borough of C___, and that his professional license was in order. These formalities being dispensed with, one of the constables requested the tale of the feral child known as Tex, explaining that howling had recently been heard late at night, bringing Tex to mind. Again, Mr. Bean seemed to hesitate, but then he nodded. After a long draught of ale he stood and struck the floor three times with his staff.

"Hear ye, hear ye, the woesome tale called 'Tex of the Dobermans.' But first, a word from our sponsors. This mythogenetic moment is brought to you by Taylor's Haberdashery of New Ontario, who commissioned this version of the tale. Remember, nine Taylors make a man, and a stitch in time always saves nine at Taylor's. And here's to this fine inn, providing a place for us to meet, and last, but not least, here's to McHenry's Pale Ale."

[Everybody in the room drank to that.]

"Once upon a time, not so very long ago, and not so very far from here, there was an old mansion on the top of a wooded hill. This mansion was largely deserted, except for two people who lived there: Doctor Victor Franken—"

"Lee," said a listener, by appearance a tinker. "His name was Doctor Lee."

"What, was he a Chinaman?" said the storyteller, smiling.

"Of course not," said the Queen's Amazon. "His name

was Bill Lee. It was only ten years ago, long after the Yellow Horde had been turned."

"More than ten years," said a constable.

"Did anyone here know him personally?" asked Mr. Bean.

"No," said the tinker. "Nobody's left of the old village."

"Well, then. May I continue?" said the storyteller.

"Yes, you may," said the Queen's Amazon.

"All right," said the storyteller. "Let's see, where was I? Oh, yes.

"This mansion was deserted, except for two people who live there: Doctor Lee, also known as Faustus, Frankenstein, and Fu Manchu, but many in this area knew him simply as Doc Benway.

"Now living in this manse with the good Doctor was Nancy Nurse, even though she wasn't really a nurse, more like a combination of housekeeper, cook, and sometimes laboratory assistant. And for all I know, her name wasn't even Nancy.

"One winter's day, a traveler from the wilds came to town. He was a scavenger by trade, but the only load in his barrow was that of a half-dead naked boy. And what a strange boy he was! His hair was long and tangled, his ears had been cropped into points, and his eyeteeth were long and sharp.

"Well straightaway the townfolk led the scavenger up to the Doctor's mansion, and on the way, he told his story:

The Scavenger's Story

"'Oi was jus' pokin' a-boot,' said the scavenger, 'when Oi comes upon a scene of mos' terrible distraction. An 'ole tribe of Dog peoples 'ad been brutally massacreed, an' their village plundered. Pickin' frew the wrack an' ruing, Oi comes upon the like of 'im, left for dead wif all the others.

"'Well Oi looks at 'im an' Oi sez to meself, 'What ho! What 'ave we 'ere, Scavenger Sam? Looks like an human boy, raised by the Dog peoples!' An' Oi dropped all else Oi's doin', an' picked 'im up an' carried 'im 'ere.'"

["Here's to Scavenger Sam," interjected one listener. "Goddess rest his soul." Everybody drank to that.]

"Just as Scavenger Sam finished his story, they arrived at the mansion. The Nurse fetched the Doctor, and Sam told his story a second time as the Doctor examined the unconscious boy. The Doctor asked a lot of questions which Sam, bowler in hand, answered as best he could.

"The boy was on death's doorstep, but Doctor Benway agreed to take him in and heal him, if such a feat were humanly possible. While Nurse Nancy cleaned and bandaged the boy in the surgery, Doctor Benway went to the study and wrote in his journal. Close-up on journal, showing spidery letters in flickering lamplight:

Dr. Benway's Journal

"'February 17th — Fate has dropped into my hands an apparently genuine feral child, a boy raised by one of the wardog tribes, if I am not mistaken by his altered ears and enhanced canines. If he survives his wounds and severe dehydration, can he ever become fully human? Has the critical threshold of language acquisition already passed? His salvation lies in my hands. I must remake him from the ground up, recreate a human infancy and childhood for him, bring him back into the fold of humanity.'

"Cut to the surgery. The Doctor stitched up the boy's wounds, and then with the help of Nurse Nancy wrapped him in swaddling, as much to subdue his feral nature as to symbolize his new infancy. There were healing salves for his body, and strange medicines to ease his mind from its animal state. His hair was shorn, and his head was shaved. Nurse Nancy tended the boy as an infant, and went so far as to expose her bosom while feeding him warm milk. This was done according to the orders of the Doctor, who stayed out of sight for the first few days, outlining the operation in his study. When at last the Doctor appeared, it was to surgically remove the boy's prepuce. Just as the Dog people had cropped his ears to make the boy as them-selves, so did the Doctor reclaim him for mankind by the act of circumcision.

"Great was the boy's rage and pain over this experience, and loud were his howls. But the Doctor's mesmerism, together with tinctures of opium and ergot ad-ministered hypodermically, brought the boy into a som-nambulistic state, a trance. Then the Doctor leaned close, and tapping his own chest, said, 'Dada. I am Dada.' He tapped the boy's swaddled chest. 'Who are you?'

"'Tex,' said the boy. 'Tex . . . filius Turrean et Rex . . .'"

"'What is his name?' said Nancy.

"'Tex, son of Turrean and Rex,' said the Doctor. 'His name is a combination of the two. He is Tex of the Dober-mans.'

"Title screen, in big letters:
TEX OF THE DOBERMANS
by Norman Bean
Presented by Taylor's Haberdashery of New Ontario."

[The storyteller paused to take a drink, and his audience did the same, spellbound by the tale.]

"The pseudo-infancy of Tex was now over, and gave way to childhood. Montage: Nurse Nancy kept her shirt buttoned in front of Tex, but she spent many hours talking to him in the human language, and soon he was calling her 'Mama Nana,' just as he called the Doctor 'Dada.' By de-grees, she became more distant from Tex, more aloof. No longer did she kiss and fuss over him, and there were periods of hungry loneliness during which his cries went unanswered. And there were times when the Doctor would walk into the room, take Nancy into his arms, and kiss her in front of Tex, a sight that made the boy whimper and gnash his teeth.

"The swaddling was removed, and Tex was truly as weak as an infant, for he could barely walk, and tired quickly. His dog traits began to surface, and he was forever sniffing at things, including his foster parents. He had done this before, of course, but with his new mobility, however limited, came an access to the more private regions of anatomy. A generous use of drugs and mesmer-ism cured him of this odious habit, in time.

"One night, Tex was awakened by the sounds of a struggle, somewhere in the mansion, and he heard Nurse Nancy cry out. Quickened by alarm, he struggled out of bed and opened the door, which happened to be unlocked. Following the sounds, he probably ran up the flight of stairs on his hands and feet, like a dog. On the second floor, Tex pushed open the door to the Master bedroom and saw the Doctor and Nurse engaged in sinful congress, at which point the boy swooned and fell to the floor in a dead faint, due perhaps to his overexertion in a weakened state, or to the timely intervention of the Doctor's curious medicines . . .

"Time passes, a montage of waking, dreaming, medicine and mesmerism. Dissolve to close-up: the Doc-tor wrote in his journal

The Doctor's Journal, continued

"'July 2nd — Tex continues to make progress in language, with regards to vocabulary, at least. His sentences are never more than three words, so it may be that his language acquisition has long since passed away and all my efforts are for naught. He speaks haltingly, with occasional yips or growls.

"'At this stage we are treating his life among the Doberman tribe as a bad dream, a nightmare from which he has awakened. In carefully measured questions, I have learned something about this tribe, and the greater Dog Clan.

"'The Doberman tribe is a part of the branch we might term Labour, a group of twenty-nine tribes that includes the

Malamutes, Boxers, Mastiffs, and Danes. The Dober-mans have strong ties to four other tribes: Shepherds, Terriers, Rottweilers, and Pinschers.

"'While discussing philosophy and religion, with an eye to converting the poor boy, I was quite surprised when he blurted out 'Virtue — Only — Good.' Probing further, I found that this is a tribal belief among the Dogs, that Virtue is the only good. A very stoical belief it seems, too, and one which is often mentioned whenever Tex talks about the endless and unceasing battles against the Rabbit, Ox, and Dragon peoples. I have learned about the Cow-boys of Ross, and the Bullmen they grow into; their leader is always one without offspring who castrates himself and throws the organs over his shoulder. But it is the Rabbit Clan that arouses a contempt in Tex, who says of their beliefs, 'Pleasure — Greatest — Good.' Then he makes chopping gestures and speaks with relish of invading enemy burrows to commit murder and mayhem.

"'Only now does it occur to me, in writing it all down, what it is that they mean. Rather than 'Stoical' as I wrote above, this tribal belief system should be called 'Cynical,' as that term originally meant one who believes that virtue is the only good! And the Rabbits, with their pleasure theory, are clearly hedonists. How has it come about that these forgotten philosophies of the venerable ancients are now fought out among the non-human tribes?'

"Dissolve to the outdoor scene, on the grounds of the estate. The Doctor was reprimanding Tex for trying to mark a tree as a territorial boundary in the dog fashion when the dull sound of sheep-bells interrupted the lesson, and they looked over to see a group of Shepherds, with a flock of Sheep people in tow. The Shepherds stopped and waited respectfully at the boundary, barking and yipping amongst themselves.

"The Doctor turned to Tex and said, 'What is it, Teddy? What are they up to?'

"'Holy days come,' said Tex. 'They pilgrims are. Go

Wilson Mountain. Star in sun.'

"Just then, the Dogs became very agitated. First they howled out loud, and then they knelt to the ground as one, even striking the legs of their Sheep-slaves to make them kneel also. They began chanting 'Tex est Rex.' Mortified, Tex fled into the house, and the Doctor chased the Dogs away.

"Cut to close-up: the Doctor writes in his journal

The Doctor's Journal, continued

"'July 13th — "Tex est Rex"? What does it mean? Is poor Teddy, as we now call him, considered the king of an extinct tribe? For if what Scavenger Sam said is true, then the Doberman tribe has been wiped out completely, by forces unknown. What a cruel twist of fate, that the changeling becomes the last of his tribe. I must see about getting him to an orphanage far away from the Dog lands. We must bury this thing once and for all.'

"It was night when the Doctor put down his pen and closed up his journal. A summer storm was coming from the south west, borne by the hot wind called Saint Anne's. Agitated, the Doctor went to Nurse Nancy's door, and quietly let himself into her room, but was surprised to find the room empty. 'Where is she?' he wondered.

"A floorboard in the hallway creaked. The Doctor opened the door, so startling Nurse Nancy that she gasp-ed. He drew her into the room and closed the door.

"'Why are you sneaking like a thief?' he said. 'You look like a child caught with her hand in the cookie jar.'

"'I . . . I was checking up on Ted,' she said. 'He had such a tantrum today, I . . . I thought . . . but he wasn't in his room . . . oh Goddess, have mercy on me, how I've sinned!'

The Nurse's Confession

"'The acting, the play-acting for Ted, became too much

for me,' she said. Close-up on her face, eyes brimmed with tears, tears running down her cheeks. 'It opened old wounds, some you know about, some you could never guess. When I first came to work for you, I had girlish illusions that you would one day fall in love with me and make me your wife.' Superimpose a montage: the desert sands and canals of Ross, the roving bestial tribes, the view from a train. 'I worked so hard to attract your affections, even gave you my maidenhood, but in the end you couldn't be burdened. Do you remember the leave of ab-sence I took, many years ago, in order to tend my sick mother? She was not ill, I did it to hide my pregnancy from you . . .'

"'Pregnancy?' said the Doctor, sitting down on the bed.

"'Yes,' said Nancy, 'and when I knew that you would not marry me, I resolved to hide my shame by going back to Tarzana. I had the baby, but never saw it, as my mother took it up and gave it to some missionaries bound for the Wastes, telling them that the mother had died giving birth. There you have it, my darkest sin . . .'

"'The child was taken into the Wastes?' said the Doctor, standing up.

"'That is why it tore my heart in two, to have you pretending such passion for me in front of Teddy, passion that evaporated as soon as we left the stage. And all to tor-ment Teddy! You cannot know how much you have tortured him. I began visiting him at night, to comfort him, and . . . yes! Yes, we became lovers.'

"'Lovers?' shouted the Doctor. He slapped her. 'Are you *mad?*'

"'He is twice the man you are,' she hissed, her hand to the red swelling on her face. 'He is an animal, he had to kill to become king. He told me of his life as the king of the Dobermans, and promised to make me queen . . .'

"'King while the tribe yet lived?' said the Doctor. All the blood ran out of his face, and he sat down, clutching at the bedpost. "'Tex est Rex,'" Tex is king, yes, it makes sense now, Tex killed the king to become the king. But, Rex was his father . . .'

"'What are you saying?' said Nancy.

"'We were only acting, but Teddy, *Tex*, has really been through all of this before. What we sublimate, the Dog people express. Dear Goddess, he has already killed his Dog-father and married his Dog-mother . . .'

Nurse Nancy gagged, gasping out, 'Doctor Benway . . . what . . . what have we done?'"

"'Merciful Goddess,' said the Doctor. "'Tex est Rex" also means "Tex *eats* Rex"!'

"Just then, Tex burst into the room and began grap-pling with the Doctor, his long fangs snapping at the Doctor's neck. They tumbled and twisted across the floor, one snarling, the other shouting. Nancy Nurse started into the fray as well, either to separate them or help one to victory. In the confused melee that followed, a window was broken and a lamp shattered. Soon the entire room was engulfed in flames. Fade out.

"Nobody knows how the fight ended," said the story-teller, "but everybody knows that the Doctor was killed, and Tex took Nancy off to the Wilds to be his queen. Well, within a year the village had fallen to the Shepherds and the Aztecs. Who knows, maybe Tex led them on? But that's another story, not fit for the inn, rather the garrison instead, to keep the watchmen alert."

"There's some that say Tex killed 'em both," said the tinker, after the applause and tossing of coins.

"Hard to say," said one of the constables. "No bodies were ever found."

"Dogs, they drag off what they kill," said the storyteller. "Or bury it, to dig up and eat later."

"Maybe the Doctor killed the Nurse," said the barkeep. "Wasn't there something sort of, *unnatural* going on in that house?"

"Yes, I heard he was buggering the boy," said the Queen's Amazon. "That's a capital offense right there. Plus all of that experimentation sounds heretically close to dabbling in black arts. What do you think, Ed?"

I could feel the heat closing in, feel them out there making their moves. Beans and rice, how nice. I wrote on my slate, "PERHAPS BOTH KILLED TEX?" and held it up for all to read. The Amazon scowled. Mr. Bean looked towards the constables and said, "What, cat's got his tongue?"

"No, his voice box was crushed by Boxers during the rebellion," said the Queen's Amazon.

"Mr. Bean," said one of the constables, "meet our visiting scholar, Ed Burroughs, from the Queen's Museum. Mr. Burroughs, meet our visiting storyteller, Norman Bean."

Ed burrows, Ed borrows, Ed burrows in ancient barrows. Of Ed, to Ed, for Ed, oh Ed! Oh Eddy Piss.

"Boxer Rebellion, eh?" said Mr. Bean, after we had nodded to each other. "I guess you're lucky to be alive. Where were you, when it all started?"

"WASTES OF ST. FRANCIS," I wrote.

•

My name is Edgar Burroughs. My title is Archivist of the Queen's Museum. My subtitle is field agent. I cannot speak, but sometimes I howl. I am afraid that I have been too much in the field of late, and hereby request a furlough for the purpose of recuperation. Living among these phil-istines, with their technological bans and sadomasochistic culture, has taken its toll on me.

When burning building, dog boy wonder. Take one out, go back for another. First body gone, second body drop. Dog boy run into the night, don't stop.

After the Aztec War, he came into the Sanfuran with a handful of Shepherds, preaching to all about barbaric hill-folk.

"See, see their telegraph cables, blades to injure the Wind. Hear, hear the moaning of the spirits as they pass the wire. Taste, taste the water that drips off of the wire, is it not the taste of blood?

"But there is more. They dig up our corpses for their necromantic arts. They hunt us for sport, exterminating whole tribes at a time, and yes, they perform hideous experiments and vivisections upon us. They think of us as sub-human, or worse.

"Tell me, what is the Way?"

"To walk and not to crawl."

"What is the Way?"

"To obey the Masters."

"Where are the Masters?"

"Gone home across the sea."

"Are we not soldiers of the Celestial Empire?"

"Yes, we are."

"Then we must fight, and continue to fight, even without the Masters."

Fight go bad. Rebellion crushed. Changeling change again. File teeth easy. Ears rush job.

The title of this story is "Tex of the Dobermans." The name of this story is "Tarzan of D'Urbervilles," but I call it "Family Reunion: All's Well That Ends Well."

•

"The very heart of the maelstrom," he said. "I take it back, what I said. It's a miracle you survived!" Is that a light, slowly dawning in your yellowed eyes, Bill?

"Bastards took his ears, though," said the Queen's Amazon.

"What animals!" said Theresa the barkeep. Or should I call her Nancy? "They deserve what they got."

I retired shortly thereafter to my room, and rose early the next day to take my leave of the borough of C___. Cognizant or otherwise, Theresa was not there beside her husband the innkeeper when he saw me off on my bone-jarring ride to the station, on the way back to the north.

But Tess, your secret is safe with me.

ALIENS WITH CANDY

The alien bought me some candy from the machine I'd been looking at. I was a nine-year-old girl from the interior, a rube in the coastal city, but I knew all about molesters, strangers who give you candy and then do something bad to you. I knew that rape was something bad that someone did to you "down there," but I thought it involved a knife. I'd been hanging out at the corner store after school, not wanting to go to the apartment yet, looking at the candy that was ruby red and shaped like a corn kernel, but faceted like a jewel.

I knew nothing about the aliens except that they'd won the war. You have to remember that this was way back before we ever hammered out the biotech protocols. There were all sorts of tensions and even some violence. The aliens mostly kept to themselves and this was certainly the closest I'd ever been to one. He looked like a tall man, over seven feet tall, but the bone-white skin of his hands at the candy machine proved he was alien. The candies sat there in the little trough, three shiny jewels, while I won-dered if aliens were even really "strangers" in that sense . . . I couldn't let it go to waste, and so I took the candies.

They were sweet like cherries, leaving a slight tang at the back of my mouth.

"Can you please help me?" said the alien in a soft hissing voice by my ear.

The social conventions of a child are strange and strong. Having taken the candy I was obliged to do some small favor in return.

"Okay," I said.

It was like I was under a spell. The shopkeeper, the worker pushing a broom, the few customers, and all the other kids looked at me like I was already dead, but they couldn't fight it any more than I could.

We walked out of the store and down the street. He didn't touch me or hold my hand but I was walking beside him.

"I'm looking for a friend's place but I've lost his address," he said. "It's a building right around here, somewhere."

We walked past the school that I hated after only two months, a place of pavement and painted lines for everything. I wanted to finish fourth grade at my old school, with the grassy field and the climbing trees and the big old library.

"I don't know the place very well," I said.

"That's a cute dress you've got on," he said. "Country fresh, straight from the interior. You new around here?"

"Yeah."

We were at the traffic light. If I just turned right, the apartment was only five blocks away. I could run.

The light changed and we crossed the street.

Down the block we came to an apartment building. It was two stories tall, with the rooms all opening on a central courtyard that could have a pool, but didn't. A stairway went up on the left in the open-air entryway, across from the bank of mailboxes. The stairs were light and airy, simple concrete steps like planks on a central metal strut, with wrought-iron handrails. It was a safe spot with no dark hidey-holes where bad things could happen.

The alien was squinting at the names on the mailboxes, his cat-like eyes peering through his glasses.

"No, that's not it," he said softly. "No . . ."

I wondered if he really was looking for someone like he said. I wondered how many buildings we were going to try.

"Not here?" I asked.

"Maybe," he said. "There's one apartment I'd like to try. This way."

That was it for me; there was no "maybe." I turned and ran out the front of the building, glancing back once to see him starting to turn.

I ran down the block and pushed the button at the crosswalk. It was a warm spring day but I shivered a few times. I felt stupid, so unbearably stupid. Everything looked the same as before, which seemed strange. I got scared that he would come running after me and drag me back.

I crossed when the signal changed. Then I got scared that he might try following me to the apartment, so I looked back every few minutes, but I never saw him.

My mother asked me why I was late and I told her the whole shameful story, which is kind of surprising. She flipped out, called the police and everything, but I didn't begrudge her doing that. The police couldn't do anything but say they'd be on the lookout.

The next day in class was almost worse. One of the strange daily rituals at that place was the students had to stand up and say, "I like myself." Down the line, each one saying it, unless someone said something like, "I hate myself."

I was crying inside but there was no way I was going to say anything to those mean kids or that fourth grade teacher who wasn't my fourth grade teacher. I hated that place, I hated my situation, and I felt bad about myself, but I said, "I like myself," and sat down.

As the ritual continued I started to wonder why I had gotten away so easily, and then I was scared that some-thing bad really had happened but it was so awful that I had blanked it out. How late was it when I got to the apartment, anyway?

Meanwhile the ritual came to a halt with a black girl who said, "I hate myself." So the teacher talked to her about her feelings and helped her work out what the prob-lem was. I can't remember what it was but I thought it was trivial compared with my unspeakable thing.

A week later my mother took me to stay with my father and finish my school year. When she hugged me goodbye I could hear her heart beating very fast, and I knew she was upset, but it was the happiest day of my life.

It was a dream come true. There was my father, a scientist-turned-farmer like so many of them were. There was my school, and my teacher. There were my classmates and my friends. I didn't tell anyone about the alien, and as I got back into the rhythm of my former life, the whole thing became a mild nightmare, easily forgotten.

But then it started to seem unreal, like I had made it up in order to scare my mom into sending me back. So I felt a little guilty, but mostly I was happy and relieved.

The place was the same old desert but now I saw it all a little differently. I could see how poor and simple we were, farmers and townies alike, compared to the city folk, but I had also seen the war damage in the city, the ruins that pocked their neighborhoods. For us the war damage was only at the military base, now a glassy crater that was miles away. Still, I could see that the area was dying, since the town had relied upon the base, but I thought it was a slow death of people moving away.

I didn't really think that my mother would come back to live in the house and reunite the family. I just felt I had been granted a temporary reprieve. Deep down I must have hoped it would happen, though, that another dream would come true, but I didn't pray for it. Maybe I should have.

The school year ended and my mother came to take me back to the coast. At the last minute I started to resist, tell-ing her how much I hated that place.

"Don't worry, we aren't going there," she said, sooth-ing me like I was still a little kid. "We're going to a different place, on the beach, and a different school."

"A different school?" I said, trying to catch up with this new information. "Is it better?"

"I think so," she said. "I hope so."

During the long drive I pestered her with more questions about the place, figuring there must be a catch. Her answers made things seem even more incredible, and I started to get that giddy feeling of dreams coming true.

It was a house, then a big house, and finally a mansion. It was not a mile from the beach, it was not five blocks from the beach, it was actually on the beach. On a private beach.

I asked her about the job she'd found. She said it was secretarial/clerical: "Writing things down, typing them up, sending them, filing them."

"Is it very far from this beach house?"

"It is in the same building."

"Mom, are you a live-in maid?"

"No, no," she said. "There's a maid, but it's not me."

"Well, who owns this mansion?"

"A very nice alien."

After hours of driving we stopped at the guard post of an alien enclave. The guard raised the gate and we drove in. There was a short entrance road leading to a stretch of beach mansions now belonging to the occupation force.

The mansion's garage had been converted into servants' quarters, with two apartments, one for me and my mom, the other for the maid and her kids. Our apart-ment had all of our stuff already in it. I put down my luggage and followed my mother into the main house.

When my mother introduced me to the owner she had to prod me to respond. She thought I was just being shy and tired, but the alien looked exactly like the one who had bought me candy. I didn't tell my mother since I hadn't seen many at all and they all looked alike.

We spent the summer settling in. The maid's three kids, two girls and a boy, were all older than me but we got along well and played on the beach just about every day. The maid herself was friendly but kind of sickly.

The summer ended and the local school turned out to be much better than the bad school.

Linda the maid died the next summer and her kids were gone the day after that — "to live with relatives," my mother said. Within a few weeks my father died when my hometown was razed during a police action. My mother wept that he had been too stubborn to get out while there was still time. A new maid with two young girls moved in.

One night my mother went up to the main house after dinner and was away all night. When I asked her about it at breakfast, she said she'd been working very late. She definitely looked tired. She got better in a few days.

The same thing happened the next summer, only this time she needed a week to get better and she seemed to lose her breath easily. I was worried about her but when I tried to talk to her about it, she snapped at me and said she was all right.

At the beginning of seventh grade I was nervous about junior high and a new school, but it turned out to be fine. Nobody ever said "collaborator," or "quisling," or any-thing like that, and I was relieved to find it was because we were all in the same boat, to a greater or lesser degree. The alien enclave had become the main economic force for the area, just like the military base had been for my old home-town.

As the school year flew by I felt a growing dread for the coming summer. All too soon the school closed and the vacation started. The days of fun in the sun piled up for me and my "little sisters" next door. The happy distrac-tion of beach balls, sandcastles, Frisbees, boogie boarding, and swimming gradually wore away my fears until I nearly forgot them.

Then in the middle of summer my mother went away for the night, and when she came back she looked worse than ever. I got very upset and hugged her, as much for her as for myself, but this simple act led to the shock of my life when I felt through our contact that her body was missing something — a breast.

A dizzy feeling came over me as I held her at arm's length. It was a terrible darkness, like that nightmare time when we'd first come to the coast. I must've looked pretty bad, since she tried to comfort me.

"Sweetie," she said, "I gave it to him. It's a little thing, really. It's nothing."

"But *why?*" I asked, sounding like a little kid.

"Let's sit down," she said.

So we sat on the couch, and I noticed the walls stopped closing in.

"This was the last time," she said in a very quiet voice. "We will be okay now."

"What do you mean, 'last time'?" I asked. "What did he take before?"

"A lung," she said, looking away. "A kidney."

"Oh mom," I said, my hands raised to cover my mouth.

"See? This is less than that, except that it shows."

"But *why?*" I asked. Trying not to cry, I put my fists into my lap and asked, "Why would he do that?"

"I don't know, really," she said.

"Why would you agree to it?"

"For you, sweetie," she said, looking deep into my eyes and patting my fist. "That's the price for living here."

"It isn't worth it," I said, which made her wince. In the past she would've gotten fiery mad at such sass, but now she was so weak she didn't. That made me even more scared. "This is what killed Linda, isn't it? What if we moved a mile from the beach, would that cost half as much? We should move even further, because you can't take much more of this!"

"When I said 'living here,' I meant living on Earth," she said. "But mainly I do it so that no alien will ever do it to you. Linda's kids are now safe for life."

I was sickened by her faith in the aliens, as well as her suicidal, maternal self-sacrifice, not to mention our position as cattle for the aliens. It made me so mad that such things were being done at all, and without my knowing, and without my consent. I think all teenagers are naturally over-dramatic, but this was really grand opera, so I stepped into my role and played the part the best I could.

I felt weird, like I was waking up from a dream. The dream was the beach house and everything that had happened in the years since that day I'd met the alien. The reality felt like I was a scared kid walking those five blocks back to my apartment, looking over my shoulder. My fears back then were right, I had led the alien to my mom. It was all my fault, but maybe I could still make it right.

When I went up to the main house it was like I had turned round on the street and gone back to the apartment building where I had escaped the alien, where he was still waiting. I went into the main house and sold my own ounce of flesh.

•

Mothers and daughters are all like this. My mother raged. "Candice, how could you do this to me? You throw away my work for you!"

I told her she was worth more to me alive.

We moved to a small house on a hilltop about five miles from the beach. I didn't have to change schools, and while we never had much money, we always had enough to get by.

The client rights movement was just beginning, and I was only a girl, but I practically wrote the whole thing myself. Nowadays masters cannot legally extract their clients to death, and top market prices are guaranteed to go directly to the client. We had been treated worse than farm animals, and I'm proud that I helped improve the human condition.

My mother lived another eight years before she finally died of the medical complications. I was able to extend her life and it was worth every day. I'd do it again, even knowing what I know now.

Maybe I was too young to do what I did, too young to

understand. I blush to admit that I thought of what I sold as being like a pomegranate, one of two that I had been born with, and yet the childish image turns out to have been more accurate than not, since the pomegranate con-tains enough seeds to start hundreds of individuals. The potential of hundreds of little sister daughter selves is limited by technology and chance to only a few dozen.

And now we are three in my house on the hill. Echo and Image each had to buy her own way out, but they could not sell an ovary like I did since that is now illegal. Besides, they are as sterile as mules, making it easy for them to do as I say, not as I have done.

We look forward to the rest of us coming "home." Shade, the oldest, is now at the same age I was when I bought my freedom. Umbra, the youngest, is the age I was when I took the candy. Those three little ruby red seeds.

MICHAEL ANDRE-DRIUSSI

WHITE JAPAN

"Aren't those difficult to walk in?" she asks over the grating crunch crunch of his wooden sandals on the white gravel.

Still walking, the young American looks away from the Kyoto Palace and into the face of the Japanese woman beside him. His dark sunglasses. He thinks, "Oh. Her." having felt a flash in his head when she stepped onto the bus twenty minutes before, a rush followed by repression and denial:

"No. It can't happen here. Not now. Not here."

But she won't be shaken, and after they tour the palace, she takes him out to lunch. Later he meets her in the park. Warm summer night. They talk for hours.

"Do you have any family?"

"No. No family," he lies. My sister in.

She takes him back to her ryokan room. He sleeps beside her on the tatami mat.

"Oh. We are so foolish, so foolish . . ."

"Don't worry," she says.

After a while, she smiles. "I first thought you were English . . ."

"Why?" he asks, self conscious of his vestigial speech impediment, his affected mannerisms.

"Your hair. So dark. And your body, so slim . . . is that the word? Slim. The only Americans I've known were Navy men, blond and . . . heavier . . ."

He sleeps and dreams of a small apartment. White. Cold; an entropic chill seeping through the walls from the snow banks outside.

•

[The English language you are able to speak?]

The gas station attendant smiles and shakes his head. [No, I am not able to speak.]

He nods. [I understand.] He takes a breath and continues.

"Which way to the highway? [the highway] I am going to [Hiroshima]."

The attendant beams and points down the street. Polite little bows.

"How far?" He holds up one finger, three fingers, six fingers. A question.

"Many," says the attendant, waving down the street.

[Very much thank you.]

[It is nothing.]

The young American picks up his bag and resumes walking through Kobe. At the highway he sticks out his thumb, slightly un-nerved by the way the cars drive on the left side of the street.

Before long, he gets a ride from a stuttering Japanese business man who takes him to the marina for lunch, and then a truck stop where he introduces the hitcher to a truck driver. The truck driver takes the young American on a circuit of the nearby cities. They have cans of iced coffee at another truck stop; the driver finds a semi-truck driver with Hiroshima license plates who is willing to take along a foreign passenger.

The first driver introduces them and bows out. Dinner at another truck stop; beer drinking with other truckers at a fourth. The hitcher wonders at these youngish Japanese truckers; the way they expose their bulging bellies to each other with pride. He is introduced to a stern looking trucker who agrees to take him the rest of the way.

Sleeping in the back of the cab, he dreams of a small white apartment so cold that his breath fogs. There is a scuffling sound at the front door. In the silence he goes to the door and listens: nothing. He undoes the deadbolt lock and cracks open the door onto an icy world of Quonset huts and tepees. A blonde girl child is huddled on the doorstep, her feet blue from the cold.

He wakes up. The truck is still, the driver is gone. Through the side window he sees a factory looming in the night with large blue letters: "MAZDA." [Mazuda.] He wonders if the driver will try to rape him and then he falls asleep again.

In his dream he is working on a tri-cycle. Knobby tires. Multiple gears. "Come to bed," she says from the next room. "I'm cold." "In a minute . . . when the trike is ready we can haul things, I can haul things. Not big or heavy things, but more than a single person could carry." He puts down the wrench and goes into the bedroom, slap-ping his hands together to warm them.

She looks up at him from beneath the sleeping mound (pieces of rug, blankets, and an open sleeping bag). Her hair, tangled and matted, looks like gold in the candle light.

•

"At long last, Hiroshima." It is a world of glass and chromium, futuristic and spotlessly clean. Blue piping. Moving sidewalks. A big green park. "Is this the right Hiroshima?" he wonders. "The place where the sun touched down forty-some years ago? Atom bomb? 'Atom bomb? Oh, you mean the other Hiroshima, Atom City. It's just down the road . . .'"

Inside the museum by the park he finds the other

Hiroshima, the famous Hiroshima. It is a large diorama of apocalypse: matchbox houses flattened and scattered; the charred and broken eggshell dome of city hall; a little red ball hanging above it all at the hypocenter.

A bus load of elementary school children floods into the museum. A thin white giant surrounded by yellow dwarves, he turns to them, wanting to say, "Hey, kids, sorry about your city . . ." but they are all smiles. [Look, an outsider man!] [An American he must be.] He has become the center of attention in the museum. Not even the life-size mannequins with their hair on fire and yards of skin hanging off their arms can compete with the young Amer-ican. "Peace! Peace!" the children happily cry, waving tiny two-finger V signs.

The children remind him of the dreams. As he looks at the other displays, he puzzles over the dream girl. "Why child? Why blonde? She said she was twenty-five. I thought she was lying. Blonde: two girls back in the states. One goes to church. The other has arms dotted with death runes, needle tracks. That woman in Kyoto was twenty five; maybe dream girl is a composite of three; like the tri-cycle."

He is outside, in the green park, walking toward the hypocenter. Once there, he turns around to find the Kyoto woman beside him. Takes her in his arms. Bites deep into her neck.

When he comes to, he is being helped up by white gloved men in blue uniforms. The woman is nowhere in sight.

"Are you all right?" asks the policeman.

[Yes, yes.] "Yes, I'm fine, thanks." [Very much thank you.]

•

On the sleeping train to Tokyo his dreams turn on the cold white apartment. A young voice shouting outside: "Jack's Hardware! Special on thermal seals! Jack's Hardware! Always an honest deal! Jack's Hardware!"

He throws on a blanket and leaves the apartment; she locks the door behind him. He sees words on the wall: ATOMATOM, CHILD BRIDE, and WHITE JAPAN. He walks to the quonset hut, to Hardware Jack. "Listen," he says to the man, "I've got a trike. I can haul for you in trade for some thermal seals. What do you say?"

•

It's a cold morning in Tokyo as he calls her up on a blue telephone. Her mother answers.

[Hello, hello?]

[Yes, Yumi Miss present is?]

[Oh. Just one moment please. Who calling is?]

[I am sorry. I don't understand. Japanese language I cannot speak.]

"Okay. I get Yumi." There is a tinny strain of muzak and then the woman he met in Kyoto comes on the line. "Hello? This is Yumi."

[Yes, this is me.]

"Oh! Your Japanese is getting so good!" [Really!]

[No, I am poor.] "I dreamt of you . . ."

"Hmmm." He can hear her smile. "Was it a good dream?"

"I'll tell you about it later. Meet me. Today."

"I have to go to work. Where are you?"

[Ichigaya at I am staying.] "Call in sick. Meet me at Mishima's favorite tomb in Aoyama. At noon."

"I can't!"

"You will."

The day is heating up as noon approaches. He buys a tall bottle of Sapporo beer from a vending machine and sips at it as he walks into the necropolis. He threads a path among the graves, glancing at a page in Mishima's novel *Runaway Horses* for directions. Beside a shady pine tree he finds the massive upright slab adorned with columns of ancient

Chinese characters. She isn't there. He sits, drinks, thinks. "Printed words in that dream. ATOMATOM, atom fused with atom, confused with 'automaton' to form a new totemic god. Of fear. That came from the museum. WHITE JAPAN is massive Caucasian migration to Japan, as victors or refugees. Or death of Japan; 'white' in Japanese is 'shiro,' sounds like 'shinu,' to die. Or Japan is becoming white, turning away from China, Westernizing. Or all three at once: foreign invasion/death/transfor-mation. That must be coming from the background. China White: a kind of heroin. Like Marianne, another death/threat. CHILD BRIDE, what is that? Referencing back to the dream itself, but isn't there a real-world cor-respondence for that one? My sister in. In. Captivity . . ."

He jumps at the snap of a twig.

[O! Pardon me.]

[No, it is nothing.]

She smiles. "I'm glad your English translation is so close to the original . . ." she holds up a Japanese version of the Mishima novel. "Otherwise, we would've gone to different places."

[Beer, do you like to drink?]

"Yes, but . . ."

[Here, please be my guest,] handing her the bottle.

[Thank you.] She sips. [Warm weather, isn't it?]

[Yes.] He points at the little grave beside the family slab. [What does it say?]

"Ahh . . . it's the grave of a young girl. A granddaughter. Her family name is Mishima."

"'Mishima' was the author's pen name, [do you understand?]" She nods, [Yes.] "I wonder about the girl buried here. Did the author love her?"

"I don't know."

He kisses her. She keeps him at arm's length, smiling. "Not here. You are so crazy! There are caretakers all around."

"There are more trees and bushes than caretakers."

"Wait until nightfall."
"Mm. No."

•

At Sanseido Bookstore he buys a copy of Ballard's novel *Crash!* which he reads on the north bound train. The wall says HEROINJAPAN. He goes inside of the white apartment. She looks sick. He says, "A stranger from the outside came today. I didn't see him, but now everybody is talking about this test. If we take it, we can get out of here." She rolls over, looks at the wall, away from him. He strokes her tangled blonde hair. "I'm sorry you feel so bad, but you'll get better and then we can take the test and get out of this place. I wonder what kind of test it is? Written or oral? Maybe an essay?"

"No, you big dope. It's not that kind of test." Then in another voice, a small voice, she says, "I'm sorry . . . I'm sorry . . . I lied to you. I'm only fourteen and, and I think I'm dying . . ."

"Thee I knew, I knew, I knew."

"'Hero in Japan': that's me. 'Heroin Japan': heroin, that's Marianne, but she's in Los Angeles. 'Heroine Japan': that's the girl in the dream isn't it?"

He is knocking around Hokkaido for his last days in Japan. Largely by accident, he stumbles into a remote village of fair-skinned Japanese. Blue eyes. The Ainu. He shivers behind dark sunglasses in the summer sun. White Japan.

MICHAEL ANDRE-DRIUSSI

MENTALLY GIFTED MUTANTS

"Jack," said Mrs. Lennart, sitting behind her desk at one end of the small room, "the school board wants to see something to justify the program."

The teenage boy known as Cryojack felt a twinge of unease. He looked up from the paperback to face his paranormal studies teacher, tucking his long sun-bleached hair behind his right ear to bare his face.

"You mean, like, a demonstration?" he asked, his mouth suddenly dry.

"Yes. Maybe you could make another ice pin . . . ?"

The unease grew larger, spreading tendrils of dull numbness down his arms and legs. He set the book aside and looked down at the table, the hair sliding forward to veil his face.

"I can't, you know that," he said. "It was hard enough to show you. I can't do it in front of crowds."

"I know, I know," she said with a sigh. She began twirling her red hair around her finger, then stopped herself. "Is there something else, something creative but not connected to your power?"

"Like what?" he asked, staring at the book cover blindly.

"You did a diorama for English class, right?"

"Yeah."

"Maybe you could build a model castle from scratch, using cardboard," she said. "Like that one, on your book. Draw up a blueprint, then build it. Make an architectural model."

"But what would — ?"

"They just want to see something," she said. "Everything is being 'means-tested,' so each member of the MGM program must produce something tangible. A demonstration of your power would be great, but otherwise, just something."

Jack looked up at the six little cubbies, one for each participant. His paraname was on one door, with TK-Oh and Cassandra as his neighbors.

"What are the others doing?" he asked.

"I don't know yet," she said. "I imagine each will be different. We only need something to show that you're not just sitting around, reading novels or something."

"I already went through all the para-books we've got," he said, gesturing at the short row of books in the bookcase otherwise devoted to the junior high school's collection of DVDs and CDs. The windowless room off the library had been used for media storage until Mrs. Len-nart's arrival the previous fall.

"I know that, but people don't know how little there is, especially in cryokinesis," she said. She tapped her finger for a meditative moment. The school bell rang the end of the period. "So you've done that work, the reading, but there's nothing to show for it. Maybe you could do a report covering all the literature?"

"No, no," said Jack, the thought of cataloguing his own inadequacies making him feel sick. He shoved the book into his backpack and chose the lesser of two evils. "I'll build you a castle."

He went out the door and saw Dee Dee waiting for him alone by a bookcase, a vision of long tan legs, short denim skirt, and blonde ponytail. Her backpack rested on the floor beside her while she idly stared at the book spines with blank incomprehension.

"Hey, Dee Dee," said Jack.

Her face lit up.

"Hi Cyrojack," she said, her braces glinting with her smile.

"Where's Jazz?"

Dee Dee shrugged, looked away.

"I don't know."

Jack picked up her pack.

"Oh, you don't have to —" she stammered, moving to take it from him.

"Please let me," he said. "It's something I can do if there's just the two of us."

"Thank you," she said, blushing and dewy eyed.

They went out the exit and started cutting across the quad on the way to his next class.

"I'm starting a secret project tomorrow and I feel like celebrating tonight."

"Yay!" she said, clapping. "Party time."

"Could we have a double-date with Sam?" said Jack, mentioning his best friend.

"Oh," she said, slowing down. "So, me and Sam again?"

"No, Jazz and Sam," said Jack. "Instead of flipping a coin, that will be her penalty for not being here this morning."

Dee Dee smiled and caught up with him.

"*If* she can make it," said Jack. "If not, then the whole thing is off."

"I'm sure she can, and Sam's a nice guy."

They entered the covered walkway intersection that had two aisles of lockers to the right. TK-Oh was heading toward them on his way to Mrs. Lennart's room, attended by his entourage of four girls, two of whom carried his backpack between them. TK nodded to Jack and Jack raised his free hand to wave back.

In the chattering knot of students by the lockers he

heard a boy's voice mutter "Groupies."

Jack thought that was an ugly word. He chose to think of them as girl friends. If the school had a prince, it was TK, and his girls were like his ministers of state.

•

That night the double date went off without a hitch and they painted the town red.

Back in Mrs. Lennart's room the next morning, Jack measured the building on the book cover with a ruler while suffering a stubborn hangover. The pictured structure wasn't a castle, really; it was an arabesque sort of fort or villa of the far future. There was a square gatehouse that was crowned by a smooth white dome and flanked by two low, square towers with connecting walls to either side. That was all. He fleshed out the plan by enclosing the courtyard with another tower and a landing pad for the giant pelicans that they rode in the science fantasy novel. He drew the plan for a model in 1/72 scale, a typical size for toy soldiers.

Mrs. Lennart wanted him to do all the work on site, so he brought materials to school and worked on it. He found a white plastic Easter egg the size of an orange and used the smaller half for the dome.

It took him two weeks to finish. It felt good to build something and stop thinking about his powers.

"Wow, Jack, this is beautiful! It looks so realistic!" Mrs. Lennart said when he showed her the final product.

"What do you think the school board will say?"

"I don't know, Jack, but it's definitely an accomplishment you should be proud of."

Looking out the open door to the library, Jack saw his best friend Sam plop down at a table and pull a textbook from his book bag. Jack hurried out to see him.

"Hey Sam, come see my secret project," he said. "Tomorrow's the official showing."

"You sure it's okay for me to go in there?" asked Sam as

he followed Jack back to the paranormal studies room.

"Yeah, come on."

"Hello, Sam," said Mrs. Lennart, looking up from her desk when they entered.

"Hi," said Sam.

"Here it is," said Jack, pointing to the model on the table.

"Looks great," said Sam, pushing his round glasses up his nose. "Wow, just like the book cover!"

Mr. Tilly, the social sciences teacher, lumbered in from the library, a bear of a man with thick glasses supported by a big red nose. Jack had never taken a class with him, but something about Mr. Tilly made him feel uneasy.

"Hello there, Sam," said Mr. Tilly. "What brings *you* to this special little room?"

Jack saw how Mrs. Lennart's eyes narrowed for a second when she saw who had entered her room.

"Just looking at this," mumbled Sam.

"Oh?" he said, turning to look at the model on its thick styrofoam base. "What is it?"

"It's just this project," said Jack, deprecatingly. It wouldn't take a psionic to detect the rising tension in the room.

"I see there's a dome," said Mr. Tilly. "Is it a temple?"

"Maybe," said Jack with a shrug. "Or a villa."

"What is this part?"

"That's the peli-pad, a landing pad for the giant peli-cans that the people ride."

"Hmmm," the teacher said, stroking his nose. "It is creative, the sort of thing you might see at a model build-ers' club." He looked at Mrs. Lennart and said, "But I think *all* the students should be allowed to build peli-pads for school credit, not just the half-dozen members of your little MGM program. Don't you think so, Sam? Anyone could do this if they had the time for arts and crafts."

The comment stung like a slap. Jack took a breath to say something, but what could he say to a teacher, even such a rude one?

"Yeah, elitism," said Sam, nodding his head. "He's got a point, mate."

Jack couldn't believe that Sam was siding with the teacher, piling on. A knife twisted in Jack's gut. Wooden faced, he left the adults to their argument. *Nothing I do ever turns out right. What's his problem with Mrs. Lennart anyway? Is it just because she's new?*

"I would like some professional courtesy from you, sir," he heard Mrs. Lennart saying as he strode off through the library.

"When you are a professional I will give it to you, madam," said Mr. Tilly.

Sam followed Jack and tried to pull him by the shoulder, but Jack shook him off.

How could he turn my best friend against me? Jack thought, blinking back the tears. *After all we've done together — or is this the thanks I get for giving him some psi drugs? I told him he probably wouldn't feel a thing. My fault for being friends with a* normal.

He left school even though it was the middle of the day. He tried to walk off his anger but it only grew strong-er. At the park near his house he saw two sparrows hopping around in a bush. He whipped out his slingshot, took up a rock, and launched it into the bush. One bird fell dead, one wing spread out. The other bird flew off in alarm, and Jack felt an empty quietness inside.

He ditched school the next day, and spent the first few hours wandering around the shopping mall. He felt sick and betrayed, a failure at fourteen. He had been in the pro-gram for four years, one year on, two years off when funding had faltered, and now this year which had been more stupid than ever. Mrs. Lennart had a recent degree in child psych and was doing "child psi" work at the school. It was a temporary job that might become permanent, and Jack liked her, but they were all flailing around, instructor and students alike. School was a joke, but the program was an even bigger joke, and he wanted out.

From the mall he went to the beach.

While walking along the pier he spotted Cassandra the precog, another MGM from his school. She was sitting alone on a bench, looking at the Pacific through silver sunglasses. With her somber clothes and black skirt, she was definitely not a surf bunny like his girlfriends. Jack made a habit of avoiding esper girls, but Cass wasn't a telepath, so he went over and sat next to her.

"Hey," he said, tipping his sunglasses.

"Hi," she said, not looking at him. Her voice croaked as though she hadn't spoken in days.

"Come here often?"

"All the time," she said. She spoke in a quiet mono-tone. The breeze pushed at her short brown hair. "But you don't. What's the matter?"

"I . . . I feel like a fake," he said, surprising himself. Such thoughts were exactly why he avoided telepaths, and here he was spilling his secrets. He locked up his greater shame at relying so heavily on the psi drugs.

"We all do," she said.

Jack panicked, thinking that she had read his mind about the drugs, but then he was boggled at how she had answered his confession.

"You *do?*" he said.

"Sure," she said. "But it is ending."

He hardly heard the second part.

"But you have a place in the Th!nk Tank."

The 'Th!nk Tank' was a well-known cartoon drawing from years earlier that characterized the popular concept of what the MGM program would produce. It showed an armored fighting vehicle manned by children: a cute esper girl with blonde pigtails sensing out the enemy location, a pyrokinetic black guy making like a flamethrower against close enemies, and a telekinetic guy riding up in the turret as the main gun.

"You have a place, too," she said, looking at him. "The tank driver."

"Only because he's not as powerful as the others," said

Jack. "He might as well be a normal."

She looked at the ocean again.

"You sound jealous," she said.

"I feel like I don't belong," he said. "My parents were so proud. They actually said it was a dream come true when I was brought into the program."

"Yes. And it was."

"One minute I was a normal and the next minute I was an MGM," he said, scuffing at some peanut shells on the pavement. "But I didn't do anything!"

"You answered the tester and passed the test," she said. "It's like, one minute you were twelve, the next minute you were a teen."

"But the test had nothing to do with powers."

"The tester looks for potential, not powers."

Jack was quiet for a moment.

"I've done my project, but maybe it's not good enough," he said.

"I know," she said.

"Well, what are *you* doing for *your* project?" he asked with irritation.

"It'll be all right," she said. "I'll kill myself."

"Don't even say that."

"Okay."

"I almost believe you."

Sitting on the bench and staring at the water, Jack thought about Mr. Tilly and became more resentful with every passing minute. He wanted to show the man a demonstration of his paranormal power, eliminate all doubts. He imagined the look on the teacher's fleshy face, his eyes bugging out in astonishment, his stammered apology.

Yeah, thought Jack, mentally savoring this delicious revenge. *But what demonstration? An ice pin? It would melt before he could see it. So he will have to be there when I build it.*

He cringed at the thought, but then he bucked up.

Yeah, he will be there, and I will make a much bigger thing — an ice spike!

Grimly happy with his new plan, Jack turned his thoughts to practical matters.

"Hey, you want to get something to eat?" he asked Cassandra.

"No."

"Okay," he said. "Well, I gotta go. I'm starving."

"All right."

"Thanks for all your help."

"You're welcome," she said.

"Are you going to be all right?"

"Everything's going to be all right."

•

He began training that afternoon, barricading himself in his room. His girlfriends kept calling because it was a Friday night, but he would not be distracted. Finally he un-plugged the phone.

The next morning he called the girls to apologize. He explained that he was working on a new secret project with no party this time; in fact, he asked them to avoid him for a week until it was over.

He practiced all weekend, emerging only for quick meals and runs to get more psionic enhancement drugs from back alley dealers.

On Monday he told Mrs. Lennart to arrange for a demonstration at lunchtime on Friday for the principal, the school nurse, and Mr. Tilly.

He went to school every day, did the work, then went home, took drugs, and practiced into the night. During each session the heat would begin on the tips of his ears, then the crown of his head would get hot. Through prac-tice he increased his power so that his whole head would heat up, and even his neck. The more heat, the stronger his cooling power.

On Wednesday he was walking alone to class when a couple of eighth graders ran up and kicked him in the ass, saying, "Cryo-baby-o. Freak."

Jack looked at the two of them laughing at him. He was used to the jocks making fun of his paraname, but these twerps seemed like an ominous sign, a problem to be nipped in the bud.

Then he caught himself and unclenched his fist.

I will not take revenge, he thought. *I will not be distracted.*

He turned and walked away, bumping into TK-Oh coming out of the office with his ministerettes in tow.

"Hey TK," he said.

"What was that?" asked TK, nodding at the suddenly quiet underclassmen. "They messing with you?"

The eyes of the younger boys went wide at this development. They had been happily playing "tweak the freak" but now found themselves staring down the barrel of the Th!nk Tank gun.

"Nah, they're just kids," said Jack, but the boys were already running away from TK's glare, fearful of his rumored ability to punch at long distance.

TK snorted and turned to Jack with a grin as he raked his dark curly hair with his fingers.

"Hey, I hear you've got a demo coming up," he said.

"Yeah."

"That's so cool," crowed TK, clapping him on the shoulder. "Good luck, man, and take care."

TK turned to go, but the four girls gave Jack intense looks of apprehension before they fell in behind TK.

•

Friday's pre-algebra class dragged on. To get the timing right, Jack went to the boys' restroom halfway through the period and downed a double-dose of psi-drugs.

The bell finally rang. He killed time, knowing that for showmanship reasons he should arrive last. On the way to the library he stopped at a drinking fountain and drank down as much water as he could hold.

Jack sauntered into Mrs. Lennart's room right after the principal. Mrs. Lennart, talking to the school nurse, looked pleased to see him. Mr. Tilly scowled his irritation at the calculated delay.

"Ready, Jack?" asked Mrs. Lennart, her eyes bright with excitement.

"Yeah," he said, dropping himself down into one of the hard plastic chairs at the table.

"Lady and gentlemen, Cryojack will now demonstrate his talent in generating a pin of —"

"Spike," said Jack, staring at the table as the heat began burning the tips of his ears. "An ice spike."

"Please watch carefully as he creates a *spike* of ice."

The top of his head heated up as if he wore a crown of fire lit by the pilot lights of his ears, and then the heat moved down his head like a knit cap being unrolled into a ski mask. When his cheeks were burning he leaned forward and spit up a small amount of water onto the table. He worked this puddle with his fingers, pinching at it and drawing it up, a trickle of sweat crawling down the back of his neck.

He coughed up more water and worked at it with both hands, building up the one-inch needle spire with additional layers. The heat was down to his neck, and sweat was running down his cheeks. He imagined he must be glowing.

It was two inches and growing. He coughed and worked it, shaking away the sweat from his eyes.

It was three inches, and now he vomited up a cup of water that seemed already an icy slurry when it hit the table.

"Jack, that's enough," said Mrs. Lennart in a soft voice.

"No, just one more."

Jack coughed up another slurry and put his breath to work, blowing on the white spire as his fingers feverishly shaped it.

It was four inches. He stopped and sat back, wiping his forehead with his short sleeve.

Mrs. Lennart had a proud smile. The nurse clapped her

hands with enthusiasm.

"Well, John, that's . . . very impressive," drawled the principal, fingering his weak chin. "Thank you for showing us . . . that."

"More architecture," said Mr. Tilly. "Some stage magic."

Jack felt dizzy.

"Now, Greg," said the principal. "Let's not be so harsh."

"What proof do you need?" asked Mrs. Lennart. "It is ice. Go ahead and touch it."

"I will not touch that disgusting thing," said Mr. Tilly.

Jack felt cold, as if his pilot light had been blown out.

"Wait, I have a thermometer," said the nurse, digging into her medical kit. "An outdoor thermometer I fixed up for the occasion."

"Yes, great idea!" said Mrs. Lennart, but Jack felt a blast of panic.

I need a distraction, he thought. *Don't look at the thermom-eter.*

"I just don't see how this thing has any application beyond being a nasty sort of parlor trick," said Mr. Tilly.

Jack felt the heat start up again, but for the first time it surged through his entire body. Sudden rage. He glared up at the teacher, wishing him dead.

"First we will establish that it is cold," said Mrs. Len-nart as the nurse put the thermometer on the table. Its plastic mounting plate had been cut away to expose the bulb, and now the bulb touched the spike's base.

"I tried it against an ice cube at home and it went down about ten degrees in the first minute," said the nurse.

"How low did it go, in the end?" asked Mrs. Lennart.

"It got down to forty-two after about three minutes," said the nurse.

"Even if he could make ice cubes, how would that help national security?" demanded Mr. Tilly.

"We just don't know yet," countered Mrs. Lennart. "It is basic research."

Jack visualized forming an ice nail in the teacher's brain, behind that scarred red nose, and he threw all of his full-body power into it.

Mr. Tilly noticed him again.

"What are you —?" he started, but his glasses suddenly fogged up.

Exulted, slightly frightened, Jack pushed harder.

"Say it," he hissed through clenched teeth.

"Jack?" said Mrs. Lennart, a worried quaver in her voice.

"Take it back," rasped Jack, feeling rivers of sweat coursing down his sides.

Mr. Tilly took off his glasses.

"Jack!" said Mrs. Lennart.

Jack knew she was right, that it was wrong to kill. Wrong to kill birds in the park, wrong to kill an intellectual bully. But he wouldn't have to kill him if Mr. Tilly would just back down in the face of a real and credible threat.

"I won't," said Mr. Tilly, wiping his glasses with a handkerchief. "You're a fake."

Jack's power was gone, as sudden as an orgasm, leaving him equally empty and weak. But in a bad way. He knew he'd made the right choice, but it was hard and it hurt.

And there was the spire of pseudo-ice, mocking him.

In impotent fury he slapped his open palm down upon the melting spike and was rewarded with blinding pain as it pierced his hand.

•

For the next few weeks Jack ditched school a lot and avoided Mrs. Lennart whenever he was at school. There was a lot of social turmoil during that time, all stemming from the ending of the national MGM program. Anti-elitist riots erupted spontaneously in several major cities. Jack's family moved out of their house and into a two-bedroom apartment, in an anonymous building, in a different part of town. Neither of Jack's girlfriends would talk to him any more. Jack cut his hair and tried to act like a normal.

A fire broke out at the junior high school and every-body

assumed it was some pyrokinetic kids lashing out, but later it proved to be normal arson.

An MGM student committed suicide, but it wasn't Cassandra after all. It was TK-Oh, the school's best and brightest, who took an overdose of barbiturates. Two of his girls tried to follow him but they were rescued in time.

At the last minute Jack went to apologize to Mrs. Lennart. He found her packing up her desk things into a cardboard box.

"Can I help?"

"No thanks, I just finished," she said, avoiding eye contact. "How's your hand?"

"Good." He lifted his bandaged right hand. "It's better."

"Your hair looks good short."

"Thanks."

He took a breath.

"I'm . . . I'm sorry," he said.

"For what?"

"Everything bad that's happened."

"It's not your fault, John."

"Yes it is," he said.

"You didn't kill TK."

"He did that because I killed the program."

"You do have to work on controlling your anger, but you didn't kill the program," she said. "That happened in Washington, starting with the election last November. Paranormal studies have fallen out of favor."

Jack took a moment to digest this.

"You mean, it's all *political?*"

"Yes," she said. "Well, maybe not all . . . there might have been some bad science going on, too."

Jack felt a pit in his stomach.

"Look, John, everything is going to be different for you from now on," she said. "You have to prepare yourself for a traditional job of some sort, since there is not going to be a psionic corps, and I don't want you making ice cubes in a circus sideshow.

"Because of the program, your basic education has suffered, and your behavioral lapses have been over-looked."

"'Lapses'?"

"Things that would have been reported to the police if you were a normal."

Jack looked at his feet.

"You have to take charge of your education and your life," she said. "It will be hard because remedial courses aren't being offered. But you can do it if you apply your-self. Make a plan, follow it, and make it happen."

He swallowed.

"What do you think?" she asked.

"Sounds like the truth."

"What will you do? What job will you aim for? Any ideas?"

"Architecture?"

"That might be wise," she said. "It will require math and science, both of which you have been neglecting . . ."

John gave her a long stare, then he moved forward and picked up the box on her desk.

"Let me carry this out to the car for you."

MICHAEL ANDRE-DRIUSSI

THE RAGNAROCKENROLL
OVERTURE

Minor Miners Digging for Cool

It was twenty years ago today that Pavel Jackovitch K'rumajin and I fell under the spell of Erebus Priestly, the King, the Original Hun Solo, the Ayatolla of Rock'n Rolla. We weren't the only ones; even in our little one-horse town of Hitachi-machi on the Central Plateau, everybody under a certain age heard the strange new sound, felt the gyrating-revolutionary itch, and swore allegiance to this new force from the South. There was no stopping Erebus, whose power was something old, something new, some-thing borrowed, and something very definitely blue.

Life before Erebus was boring and monotonous: there were tumbleweeds; there was permafrost; there were three or four alphabets to memorize; there were reforestation workgangs. There were radios, but they were mostly big and "for official use only." Stories about savage Southern cults seemed to exist only for oyai to frighten their children with. But then Erebus came. He rocked our town to its foundations, cut down all the oyai that stood against him, sending Everboy's Ma and Pa down to the chthonic depths of Heartbreak Hotel, and then rolled on to the next town, scattering portable radios in his wake.

That was an exciting time, and we were all drunk on the sudden freedom, but it was a dangerous time, too. No room left for solos, Everboy was in a band, every band battling it out on the small scale just like it was happening on the Big Stage. And I mean "band" in both senses of the word: music men and merry men. Black leather and a sneer were mandatory, so were tribal hairdos, from slicked back to spiky. You never knew if the next malchik's case had a Degtyarev "guitar," with enough 7.62mm power to wipe out the local militia in a single burst, or an electric guitar, with the power to capture the imagination and burn the brain. And that's what it always comes down to, in the end: slaughter or slavery.

So there we were, physically digging the ruins, mining for silos, and spiritually digging the received wisdom of King Erebus. We needed a name, so I came up with "The Quarrymen," seeing as how we were into rock, digging, and ordnance. At first we were four: me, Pavel, Pyotr Ichi-ban, and Stu, but after a couple of years, Yuri disbanded his "Rebels" to join us. In our digging, we would uncover priceless gems of forgotten knowledge, and strange thoughts would come to us. We fed on tales and legends of the great Alexandros Philipovitch, the malchik of Macedon who rocked the world to her knees with his three droogs and his genius Aristotle; and Peachboy, with his three animal friends, sailing forth to sack Hindia from the East . . .

Don't tell me, dear reader, that you have forgotten Peachboy, the hero of Xipango?

THE TALE OF PEACHBOY

Long, long ago, there was a giant peach. One day, it gave birth to Momotaro (alias Peachboy), who quickly grew up into your typical hero of old: strong, healthy, courageous, polite, and generous. Once grown,

Peachboy set out for the Isle of Demons (a.k.a. Hindia) to subdue the oni-demons who had been plundering villages along the coast.

Along the Way, he met Sirius the Dog, who said,
"Momotaro, Momotaro,
Won't you please
Give to me
A dumpling from your hip pouch?"
To which Peachboy answered,
"I will grant you that request
If you join me on my quest."
The Dog joined, and then they were two.
Along the Way, they met Phoenix the Pheasant, who said,
"Momotaro, Momotaro,
Won't you please
Give to me
A dumpling from your hip pouch?"
To which Peachboy answered,
"I will grant you that request
If you join me on my quest."
The Pheasant joined, and then they were three.
Along the Way, they met Homunculus the Monkey, who said,
"Momotaro, Momotaro," et cetera.

To which Peachboy answered with the standard contract. The Monkey joined, and then they were four.

Together they sailed across the Demon Strait to the Isle of Demons. There they engaged in fierce fighting, using all the tricks they could. They kicked the kopeks out of the oni-demons, looted all of the fabulous treasure, and sailed home in triumph, thus ending the tale of Peachboy.

•

It became clear to us that Erebus was playing out the Pied Piper scenario, a hip version of "Hun solo, mondo destructo." Deep down in our womb-tomb, we were dreaming up something much bigger. Pavel said to me, "Ivan Fridrickovitch, we are living on the geopolitical pivot of the world! With the right Rock and the right Roll we rocken could conquer all!" showing that he'd digested the genius of Mackinder.

And I said, "The key is emptiness and fullness. We must icky to the people, win their hearts and minds over to our cause. Our enemies, we must break their hearts, break their minds, and send them down to Hotel. To win a battle without bloodshed, that is the best Way," quoting the genius of Sun Tzu that swam through my open mind, pos-sessing and caressing me.

You see, in our search for the crude weapons of mass destruction we had accidentally discovered the wellspring of the King, the subterranean currents of esoteric know-ledge. Behind Erebus the crafty young Hun we found Sun Tzu, the crusty old Han. Here was the secret formula: "borrowed," yes; "old," incredibly so. But we still had to work out our own true "blue" and "new," and as the fighting on the old plateau was too fierce for our little five-some, we made a plan for to set out to the decadent East, source of magic and sunrise.

Initiation in the Underworld

For a new start, we needed a new name. Other bands had no respect for us, Everboy knew he could whup the ko-peks out of the Quarrymen, and sometimes they called us names, like "oyai" (on account of how the archaeological dust in our hair made us look old, plus the fact that all oyai were dogmeat in those days) and "silver fish" (because of all the books we'd uncovered and "eaten"). So we figured we'd teach them a lesson and call ourselves the Silver Beatles, seeing as how we had a plan to "beat-all" of them into a gory pulp. Plus, Silver like Mister Moonlight, watching over our nocturnal missions.

Right. So, off we ickied to the East, to Old Sony City, where we had some unexpected inside help, your basic Tarpeia, you know, the young chick that goes crazy over boys in black and unlocks the gate to the city to let them in. But I'm getting ahead of myself, and must begin at the beginning:

HOW THE BEATLES GOT THE BLUES

After a lot of haggling with the Sony zemstvo, we agreed to the terms (no bank jobs, no bombing, and no kidnapping within city limits for the duration of the gig) and were quickly booked for a little thiasus, the usual booze and fornication thing. So we showed up at the place in our battered old tarantas, set up the Equipment, and since we had some time to kill before the gig, we went poking in the local ruins. It was dark already, so we had torches, but they kept flickering like they were about to go out.

We'd hardly gotten into the ruins, maybe a verst or so, when this bird sort of hissed at us from a doorway. I thought, "Oh yeah, here's a piece. I wonder how much?" and I nudged Pavel, but instead of grinning, he just sort of stared. Spooked.

At first I thought the chick was dark, you know, a shade of brown, but as Pavel and I got closer and the torchlight touched her, we could see that she was actually blue-skinned.

"Why did you call us?" said Pavel, all nervous as a virgin, a cherryboy.

"Why did you call me?" said this blue babe, all cool and mysterious. Her face was pretty, but her mouth was big and she had snaggle-teeth.

"We want to beat King Erebus," said Pavel.

"Hey Baby Blue," I said to her. "How many of us can you take?" (I was feeling pretty etchy, I'll admit.)

She looked at me with this sly smile and said, "Eventually all, but for now I will take one of you." The she turned back to Pavel. "Who will it be?"

Ugh, those teeth were pretty bad, pretty grotty all right. Here was a candidate for the old paper bag-over-the-head trick, and I lost interest. Detumescent, you might say.

Pavel looked kind of sick when he called Stu over. "Hey Stu, in the mood for a quick touch of the cunny?"

Poor Stu, he was game.

"Doggie-style, tomodach," I told him by way of advice, and gave

him a slap on the back.

Before she led him away, Baby Blue said, "In your hometown you will be contacted by an agathodemon, a genius who will help you on your quest. But for now, while you wait, explore the basements of this temple."

"Creepy chick," I said when they were gone.

"Cynosure," said Pavel, sotto voce.

"Yeah, what a dog. Did you see those tusks?"

"Kopek. Not 'dog,' you penocephalus, 'guide.' Think 'Polaris,' dig it?"

"Rocken go to Hotel," I told him, but I was relieved that he had recovered himself.

Pavel whistled the others over. "Come on, Stu's playing and paying, so let's check out this temple."

Sure enough, in the dark dusty basements we found our Blue, which turned up in the form of eldritch ordnance. Most of it was biochemical: vials, bottles and drums of mysterious liquids; aerosol canisters on which idiot-gram instructions had half-flaked off; and masks worthy of any tribal fetish. There were also rifle-like devices, which could induce epileptic seizures by way of flashing light. In the pharmaceutical chest we found a gas that so stimulates the heart that anybody over the age of thirty dies of a heart attack. (This was undoubtedly the main agent used by Erebus to "break hearts," and known by the Southern Tribes as "Shake, Rattle, and Roll." We called it "Rollover and Die," or just "Rollover.") And there were other things we could not yet fathom at all.

After a while, Stu came down and found us in this sorcerer's workshop. I said, "Hey Stu, how was it?"

"Great, tomodach. The best." His grin became kind of puzzled. "She said all sorts of rocken weird stuff, though. She come down here?"

"Naw, we haven't seen her," said Yuri. "What, you pass out or something?" We all laughed.

"Yeah, I guess I nodded off. When I woke up, the bird had flown. . . ."

"So what'd she say that was so strange?" said Pavel.

"'I know what it's like to be dead,' 'lay down all thought, surrender to the void,' stuff like that."

Pavel got all jerky again, and it was time to go, so we hid our new cache and went to the gig. And that's the story of how the Beatles got the Blues.

•

After a few hard day's nights of experimentation on ourselves and others, we found the proper mixture of essences, vapors, and memes within that Pandora's Stockpile. Some of the old stuff is pretty nasty, like mean Mister Mustard, which will tear your lungs out in a second, or ruin them so that your oxygen-starved blood runs blue. (I always figured that was what made Baby Blue so blue, but Pavel said she was born that way.) We selected an array of more modern mixtures, which offered a wider variety of vectors as well as being more subtle in effect: Spenglerian spirochetes, Ionescoan rhinoviruses, Burroughvian bacteria, and all that. But to be honest with you, our controlled substance of choice was colorless, odorless, and tasteless; we would secretly dump it into reservoirs, and within a day or two the population would be under our sway.

As for Old Sony City, we hammered them good, we hammered them hard. Pyotr kept driving the beat as we rocken rolled over the local militia and anybody else stupid enough to get in our way. They never knew what hit them, and they were ours before we knew it.

But sack and burn, loot and plunder, all that was getting kind of old. On the Big Stage, Erebus had retreated back behind the rocken Wall, trying to consolidate power, or at least age gracefully. Roving was out; consolidating was in.

All this change brought strain to our merry band: Pavel, who often showed a somewhat mystical bent, felt that five was an unholy number, and pressured Stu into leaving. A few weeks later poor Stu died of a brain tumor, and we couldn't help but wonder if our biochemical experimentation hadn't been the cause, if not the final straw.

We came back to our old stomping grounds and laid in

for a heavy siege. Pyotr defected early on, but we took Kaltso Zvezda, artillery and signalman of the "Hurri-canes." This last change left us in the form by now familiar to all. Around that time, we got a real manager: Baby Blue had promised us an agathodemon, and while other people called him a fairy, we always called him by his name, B'riah. He was the best vizier in the world, better even than Alexandros' Aristotle, and he took us straight to the top. We were definitely in with the in-crowd of the shady underworld, the intellectual underground.

The Golden Reign of the Fabulous Four
We climbed up the levels of success, from cramped under-ground clubs, through the spacious halls, before achieving the Big Stage of stadiums and arenas. We conquered and secured the Central Plateau in about four years, and radio-air superiority played a big part. To quote the hoary Han: "An ancient scroll of military order says, 'Words cannot be heard, so cymbals and drums are made. Owing to lack of visibility, banners and flags are made.' Cymbals, drums, banners, and flags are used to focus and unify people's ears and eyes . . . so by using drums, cymbals, banners, and flags, you should take away the energy of their armies, and take away the heart of their generals."

The Beatle Empire was established after the Armistice, and our only serious rivals were some kopek-heads who called themselves "The Rolling Stones" (the idea being a cross betwixt thunder, meteors, and balls, to put it bluntly). For a time I was afraid that their name came from the old Han, for at one point he writes "When people are skillfully led into battle, the momentum is like that of round rocks rolling down a high mountain, and this is Force," but this is undoubtedly giving the Stones too much credit. We called them "the Clones" for a while, seeing as how they were patterning themselves after us, but later we dropped that epithet, so as not to anger new allies. (As it is said, "Do not bite the hand that feeds.") There were five of them, Mack the Knife, Keith the Thief, and the rest, that still harry our domains to this day.

"Not to worry," said Pavel. "They are five. The dark forces they now call collect will one day soon reverse the charges." And he would go on about the sacred four: hearts, clubs, spades, and diamonds. The hearts were the people, to win over or send to Hotel; the clubs were Kalsto's drumsticks, signaling the followers to twist and shout; the spades were for digging, be it Rock, ruin, or grave; and the diamonds were our continuing enrichment, materially as well as spiritually.

By the time a band gets to the stadium-gig circuit, it is too big to be just a "band" anymore. The two directions it can icky are into a religion or into an army. We opted for religion, trying to head off the Stones, and launched our Rubber Soul campaign. We had been in touch with this secret Gnostic group, the Pneumatikoi, and from their notions of the Pneumatics (the enlightened, which we considered ourselves), the Psychics (those who can be enlightened) and the Hylics (those so matter-dominated that they are beyond salvation) we got a lot of the elements for psychedelic warfare. It is not such a far jump from "psychics versus hylics" to the more plebeian "hip versus square," and the more layers to the signal, the more heads you will turn.

The Stones countered our gnostic gospel with "Get Off of My Cloud," like they were really Thunder Gods themselves.

"They're digging their own graves," said Pavel.

He seemed to be right, but who could suspect that they were digging his as well? The next season, they fired off "Satisfaction," aimed at destroying confidence in our rule, and "Paint it Black," which was definitely moving into the camp of the Elder Gods. Then disaster struck; there was that "auto accident," with all of its conflicting images of suicide and happenstance. I read the news that day, and saw the photograph. They blew his mind out in a car. One sniper or two? Magic bullet? We had to cover it up, deny that it happened so as to avoid mass hysteria, but privately the verdict was murder. Pavel would never have killed himself. We suspected the Nizaris, the hashashin of Mount Alamut in Caspia, but could do nothing overt about it.

Of course, it was a difficult situation, but we were able to call in a favor from the Xipangu Clone Arrangers, and they delivered "Pavel Tsu" within a week of the death of the original Pavel. I'm not sure how they did it, whether they actually grew an identical homunculus, or if they used surgery and training on a devotee, or something else entirely. And I don't want to know, having long since learned the burden of secrets. Judging by results, Pavel Tsu is as good as the original, just a tad more mystical and a lot more serious about it. I even called him "Mr. Serious" one time as a joke, and he looked at me, surprised-like, and told me he couldn't get it up no more. Well, that would make any malchik as serious as the Dog Star.

Not wanting to tempt the fates, the Beatles decided to stop touring, and instead we led our legions from the acropolis in Hitachi-machi. We had followers numbering hundreds of thousands, and secretly controlled dozens of "independent" bands that looked to us for guidance and helped keep the Beatle Empire under control. Undisputed spiritual leaders of the known world, with only the sinister heresy of the Stones to stamp out. I took on another wife, in shameless imitation of Alexandros and Roxana. First wife Cynthia was a real oni about it, and some of the followers were superstitious about Mari's sky-blue eyes, calling them cat's eyes, but things gradually settled down.

The Beatles shifted from religion-mode into army-mode, to get as far away as possible from the sacrilegious ground zero of the Rolling Stones. The codeword was "Sergeant Pepper," a stern figure of authority, a secular counter to the sacred nature of salt, as well as a veiled threat, "to shower with missiles." We offered short-term, limited amnesty for defectors ("Lonely Hearts") and hinted darkly at the annihilation to come.

The Stones responded with "Their Satanic Majesties Request," a full-scale revolt. After all this rocken time, the cards were finally on the table for Everboy to see. The insurgency was still being waged and countered on the levels of propaganda and espionage. Followers on both sides clamored for an open engagement, a battle of the bands, a naked contest of wills, but we were chary of meeting the psychopathic, suicidal Stones, especially at the battlefield of their choosing: Moskov, the old capital.

No doubt they chose Moskov in anticipation of our continued western expansion. The Han says, "Good warriors cause others to come to them, and do not icky to others," so we made a show of being taken in by the ploy, and with massed forces began sweeping west. The Stones responded by drawing all their forces into the duchy, no doubt flattering themselves as strategoi. "Appear where they cannot icky," says that crusty clerk of Cathay, "head for the place where they least expect you," and so at the last minute we turned south at the Ural-yama, slipped between the Aral and Baku Seas, punched through a weakly guarded flank, rocken rolled over all in our path on the way to Hindia, where, much to our surprise, we were welcomed as avatars, incarnations of Hindi gods.

It turns out they already had these old-time shrines to each of us: me, Pavel, Yuri, and even Kaltso. The names were a little off ("Iohn," "Pavl," "George," and "Ringo"), but the shrines pre-date the King himself. The natives knew all about Pavel's recent "reincarnation," and took it as a sure sign of his divinity. What a boon that was, to cap-ture an entire sub-continent without even a fight. Like Alexandros solving the Gordian Knot by cutting it, but even better, since all we had to do was appear. Alexandros had to proclaim himself a sun god; these people did it for us.

Those shrines were mysterious, to the point of making us kind of religious. We had gone further than Peachboy, we had succeeded where even Alexandros the Great had failed, we had rocked the world, and the earth had moved.

Stand Down, Sgt. Pepper

Needless to say, the Stones were not at all amused by our feint and counter-thrust, nor by our being heralded as Lords of Light, and it is likely that they are ultimately re-sponsible for the death of B'riah. I am not at liberty to give details, but his "suicide" bears all of their marks.

That the world seethed with unrest was expressed through all the hype about a looming "Final Battle of the Bands." The common people on both sides wanted it to happen, regardless of the consequences, and to this day they persist, like rival factions at a dogfight, trying to get the mastiffs to keep at it until one of them is sent to Hotel.

Back to the magical history tour: the next season, Mack the Knife tried another tactic, and invited us to an event he called "the Circus," a sort of military Olympic Games. Now there was no way that the Beatles were going to go to an event sponsored by the Stones, for all of the obvious reasons, but I began to toy with the idea of going by my-self.

It was the spell of Hindia, that ancient religious thing, the shock of seeing a weathered shrine that was dedicated to me decades before my birth. I fell for it. I, Ivan Fridrickovitch Lenin, immune to Nihilistic viruses, Solipsistic spirochetes, and Fluoridated water, had fallen for one of the oldest in the book: Delusions of Godhood. I saw my-self as the Genghis, "the one sent by fate," "the mighty one of the heavens." Like a combination of the Hindi Siva and Buddha, where once I had offered war, now I would give peace and love. I was the Sun King, and as such, I thought myself invincible.

I ickied to the Circus, man solo. A mistake that nearly cost me my life.

The stage was set for a human sacrifice. They had me front the Super Band, and I could tell that at the orgiastic climax of the act I would be cut down somehow. I wasn't sure whether it would be a Nizari bullet to the brain, an "accidental" electrocution, or ritual strangulation, but I could sense it lurking there, so I launched a preemptive first strike with my secret weapon, "Yer Blues," a Spen-glerian spirochete that immediately causes depression and dysfunction. (I had it in a hollow tooth.) Mack the Knife countered with "Sympathy for the Devil" in response, trying to regain control, and I've heard that it was the most inspired performance of his career (due in part, no doubt, to the effects of the spirochete), but I can't say for myself, since I escaped the place in the confusion.

You would think that such a close call would've cured me of my godhood-delusions, but no, it only served to reinforce them. I mean, I had managed to escape, hadn't I?

Even though it was the time of diamonds, the golden age, the arrival of the blue meanies and other deliriums proved that our years of biochemical spirituality were beginning to catch up. Pavel latched onto the idea of a new branch of service, a love army of redistribution, the Apple Corps.

"Why 'apple'?" I said. "Why not 'heart,' or 'love'? All you need is love."

"It's for Her," he said, leaning close in, sweaty and wild-eyed. "Five pointed star, the seeds at the core, it's Her symbol, Her number . . ."

"Who, your wife?"

"You baka!" he said. "Who do you think resurrected me and stole my manhood? Who do you think took my hammer with her sickle? She's angry now, it must be some-thing . . . crab-a-locker fish-wife, pornographic priestess . . . could the 'anti-matter' doctrine of the Gnostics be a cipher for 'anti-mother,' just as the search for 'dark matter' was a yearning for the 'Dark Mother'?"

"Yeah, all right tomodach." He was in the grip of a screaming blue meanie, that much was obvious, but the Corps idea had some merit, so we tried it out.

What a disaster that proved to be. We offered the peons love, but they wanted gold, and they nearly cleaned out the coffers. The more we lost, the more Pavel seemed to relax, as if we were somehow paying off a debt, but after a while the rest of us put a stop to the welfare business.

Everything was going to Hotel at about that point. The Beatles, having beat all, were no longer a band but a group of individuals, heading for internal warfare. Maybe it was lucky that I was in my "Love All" stage, because I gathered them 'round and said, "Stand-down, Sergeant Pepper, the whore is over, the enema vanquished. The time has come to talk of counter-suits and kings:

> *"In days of yore, the Genghis four, descended from the khan,*
> *Without a plan held all the land betwixt the twilight and the*
>   *dawn.*
> *In such a way, perhaps today, if there be no objection,*
> *We should dis-band, and each take land, avoiding unseemly*
>   *secession."*

And so we did. Pavel Tsu became the Dawn Khan by taking Cathay and all lands east; his capital is out on the isles of Xipangu, in the old capital of Shinkyo. Whether homunculus or devotee, he returned to Xipangu after all. I took Manzi and lesser Hindia, earning the title Morning Khan. Yuri got Hindia, became Noon Khan. Kaltso as Twilight Khan took the Far West, which he renamed Summerland, and is building his capital from scratch at a fertile spot by the Euphrates.

The Rolling Stones saw this great division as an opportunity for insurrection. At a thiasus for the Nizaris at Mount Alamut, the Stones and their elite guard of Hell's Angels (meaning, something like Hotel's bellboys) actually succeeded in a human sacrifice on the stage. The event was filmed, and served them as a recruiting tool, but those kopek-heads are just a fringe group. To us they are like a flea biting an elephant.

We gave the title of Great Khan to Erebus Priestly, in recognition of his pioneer work, and left him to his citadel in Cathay, incorporating him as a powerless figurehead to keep him out of mischief. In Pavel's cartomantic vision, Erebus became the Hierophant of the 22 major enigmas. (He finally up and died last year, but the bloated corpse wasn't even cold before a new Erebus, this one called Castrati, rose up to take his title. Pavel takes this as a bad omen, an alliance with the dark forces from within our boarders within our borders, but who can take it so seriously? Just Pavel, Mr. Oh-so-Sirius.)

And that's the end of the story. It's now Beatle Year 12, five years since Utopia was expanded into four-part harmony. Our mutual defense pact ensures safety and stability for the foreseeable future. I've come down of my Godhood trip, arigato ne, partly due to the sobering fact that Hindia is the land of ten million shrines. No doubt there are several shines to Alexandros, and probably even one for Peachboy, somewhere. I do still believe in the old Pax and Amor: terrorism and hate crime have been, and will continue to be, severely punished.

So, my little brothers and sisters, it is time to face the facts. Our enemies are not infernal gods against whom we must jihad, but mad dogs to be put down when they come to our village. I trust that the continued practice of public burning for these unfortunate vectors will be enough to quench your zeal, and that there will be no more cries for the Big One.

You may say that I'm a dreamer, but nothing's gonna change my world.

THE END

[The following is handwritten.]

iv found this book an pen heer, hid in plain site. hard 4 me to reed thu karakters of thu khan, but i think i get most uv it & ill try 2 finish it. 4giv my spelin.

i am called Linus, but i think i must be 4Everboy. & this story iz thu only 1 i know, bout how thu Big Show finaly came.

in thu 17th Year of Beatles, morning khan Ivan Lenin

wuz thu first 2 fall. shot down, He wuz, & Mary held Him. didn rize up agin, so i ges Jipan Klone wuz no lunger frend. then His statues fell, the sun set on His reign, & Everboy went to Hotel when thu Nitefolk came.

all thu otherz fell 2, i ges, but i donno cuz theez daz nuz travels so slo. mebee They R stil fiting. sumtimes i heer thunder, sumtimes i get reel sik. mebee thu war iz over & bof sides lost. its bin 2 R 3 years since khan Lenin died. i herd uv 1 imortul, tide 2 a weel that makes thu Great Roll ukros thu sky evernite, & uv another imortul chend 2 a Great Rock ware a vulcher eetz hiz liver everday, & a 3rd imortul who pushes a Great Rock up a hill, but it makes the Great Roll bak down evertime. thez 3 mebee thu Beatle-khans, i donno. i hop not.

iv just seen a face i cant forget the time R place when we first met. she sez her name is Liv, so I kud marry her & be Livthrasir, anuther way uv saying Liv-husband. falling yes i am falling & she keeps calling me back again. she sez she lost her baby Erebus, named after the King. her mama are ful, she let me drink her milk, she sez our suns wil riz to lite these Darklands. we eet aples. She calls me Yryn-ai-togon, a funy name. we go now.

IT'S A LONG ROAD
TO THE SKY TRAIN

The biodome was on fire, but that did not halt the looters.

Young Marika stood on the downtown street in her Marie Antoinette Bo-Peep uniform, watching in numb shock as the intruders emerged with fresh meat from her dog farm. There were child-sized Greys, towering Nordics, scaly Reptilians, stomping robots, twitchy mutants, and Saturnians with glowing discs around their pale bald heads. Marika had been outside a few times in her life, but now, with her elderly mother sobbing on the sidewalk beside her, she knew she would not go home again.

She felt the big world expanding around her like an inflating balloon, and a new fear rose within her. Though twenty-two years old, like a child she clutched at her goldilocks and tugged. *Where will we go?* she wondered in despair. *Where* can *we go?*

"Bad news," said a passing hybrid who had stopped to look. Shifting his bulky backpack, he turned his alien/human eyes to the curvaceous blonde and her bony mother. "You have nothing but the clothes on your backs? That is no good. You need stuff."

"Dey is lootin' da place," said Marika, determined not to show the fear suddenly coursing through her.

"They are hungry," said the hybrid patiently.

"Even da robots?" asked Marika, her pale face blushing with anger.

The hybrid waved that aside. "You need to go back in. Find a suitcase, or use garbage bags, and fill them with cigarettes, booze, high value items like that. I will guard your grandmother for you."

Distrustful of his offer, but wanting to use his dark menace to her advantage, she said, "No, I want ya should help me inside da place."

"As you like," he said.

At first the stream of looters impeded their way, but when the hybrid drew his shimmering knife, the stream parted for them, just as Marika had thought. Inside the dome, the familiar sight of Main Street further calmed her. As they went around the Hanging Tree she tugged on her earlobe to aid her planning process. She and her mother could not stay, they must go somewhere. She realized with a start that there was only one place, the same place so many of her relatives had gone to. With growing resolve she salvaged what she could from her despoiled home, and when they came out again Marika was relieved to see that her mother was still there.

"Come on, mamma," she said. "Time to get up an' carry stuff."

The woman did not react.

"Well," said the hybrid. "I should be going."

"Hold up," said Marika. She set down her bags and began digging through one. "I should give ya sumpin' for ya help — how 'bout a bottle? Dem's heavy an' I wanna trade 'em first."

"No thank you, I was glad to help."

"I hate to owe anybody," she said, thrusting a bottle of vodka into his arms. "Here. Now we's even. So where ya goin'?"

The hybrid started to hand back the bottle, then accepted it with a pained laugh that showed his shark teeth.

"I'm going to find work at the Sky Train."

"Hear dat, mamma? He goin' da same place we goin'. Hey, I axed ya ta get up, now get up." As the elder began to slowly rise, Marika told the hybrid, "We got family out dere — Uncle Sugar, mebbe more. I hear it's far — ya gonna take da train?"

"No, the maglev hasn't been running from Liboweier for some years now."

He tried walking away, but she doggedly followed, tugging her mother along. Now intently focused on the hybrid, Marika noticed that his rigid backpack was made of wood, something like a small chest of drawers or a miniature armoire, filled with drawers of different sizes.

"No, Marika," mewled her mother. "Let's git back. Someone will come."

The street ahead was bustling with aliens and humans going about their business, unaware or unconcerned about the situation at the biodome.

"Ain't nobody coming," said Marika. "We can't stay — 'member Slow Moe?" The older woman moaned in grief. "Dat's right, he done died outside. We gotta leave da city."

"But I's scared. It's big, too big . . ."

Marika felt her own agoraphobia creeping back, the city threatening to expand around her again. Fighting it, she squeezed her mother closer.

"Don' be afraid," she said. "Look, dis street's just like Main Street, only bigger. We've seen dem on 3V. An' all dese aliens, we've prolly met near every one of dem, since everyone visits da biodome. An' look, see doze Ay-rabs, doze Injuns, an' dem Chinee? More visitors to da dome. So it's just like da dome, dese streets and dese people. Da size is bigger, but we's only in dis little bit."

Her mother seemed to calm down, no longer holding them back. Marika was able to speed them along until they caught up with the hybrid, who grudgingly agreed to travel with them.

At first the equatorial humidity of the African coast was a novelty for Marika, but all too quickly it became an oppressive soup that she trudged through. After an hour of this, she spotted a fast food restaurant she knew from 3V commercials. Her stomach growled and she led the way to the General Gao's Chicken.

As the trio approached the restaurant, a beggar sat up to accost them.

"Do mine eyes deceive me, or is this Marika of the American Habitat Park?"

"Yeh, dat's right," said Marika, happy to be recognized. "An' dis is my mamma, Oosa." The beggar was a Chinese woman with obvious mutations — her skin was partially pebbled in patches, and her messy black hair had a number of fleshy tendrils like pale worms.

"But what are *you* doing out here, so far from your ancestral home?"

"Biodome done got burned up."

"Burned? Oh, terrible, terrible. It signals the end of an era. I hate to bother you under such trying circumstances, but could you give me some food?"

"Whatcha name?"

"Forgive me, purest of pure ones, this tainted one is called Trash."

"Okay, Trash, how 'bout I hire ya for a long trip?"

"To where are you travelling, purest?"

"Sky Train."

"Sk — Sky Train?" stammered Trash. "All the way to Tansangniya?"

"Ta Kilimanjaro."

"To Qilimazhaluo-shan," said Trash in wonder, shak-ing her head slowly. "That is halfway across Feizhou."

"Yeah, long way. Like I said."

Trash gestured Marika closer. Marika squatted down.

"Purest, forgive me, but is yon hybrid also in your party?"

"Yeah, his name's 'Duke.'"

"O purest, this is dangerous, do you not know?"

"I do. If ya come wif us, ya can guard me."

Trash laughed.

"True," she said. "I am tainted — he would never eat me. Still, it's a long way. Where is your car, purest?"

"Ain't got no car."

"No car! But purest, how will you go?"

"On foot. Get rides."

"Getting rides for only one or two persons is one thing, but it seems less likely with the three you have, and even less with four, should I be added. Purest, would you con-sider hiring a taximeter cabriolet?"

"Sure, if'n we could pay da price. Where dey at?"

"I know this man, a driver who owns his car. I think he would be interested in a job like this."

And so they came to meet Driver Danesh, a cyborg taxi man. Danesh told them the trip would take at least eight days, and pointed out that accommodations along the way would not be free. He mentioned cities Kahawa, Cipla, and Gazprom, names that were like wondrous fables to Marika. Mother Oosa came out of her stupor then, an-nouncing that they were "on tour," and she negotiated with Danesh about giving paid visits to towns and cities along the way.

"We'll call it, 'A Evenin' wif Marika, Last o' da Bio-dome,'" she said. "Or make dat 'Tea Time,' dependin' on da hour. An' I'll get up on da stage, or on a box, or even on da hood o' da car, if it come to dat, an' I'll give a little speech like dis — Ladies an' gentlemen, I's sure you know dat I is Oosa, an' dis here's my daughter Marika. Many or most o' ya has visited our home, da dear ol' biodome, where us folks has lived fer generations beyond countin'. An' now, fer da first time, we is come to visit you."

The money raised this way would form the basis of Danesh's fee.

Danesh realized they were asking him to drive on spec. He considered carefully, the fingers of his metal hand drumming on the counter.

•

The first day they drove, made their stop, did the job, and slept a few hours before starting out again. This set the pattern, and even though one town was Chinese, another was Indian, and a third was Russian, still, they were all pretty much the same, despite the bank, the pharmacy, or the mosque at the center of each. They kept gaining eleva-tion as they drove east into the heart of the continent. On the fourth day they were 2,000 feet above sea level, where the air was thinner and drier. That night Marika saw stars for the first time.

But as they got further from the coast, the work itself became harder. Marika was just an object, but by stages she went from being an object of beauty to being an object of scorn. She met each threshold with greater unease, but in the end she always agreed — first to pose nude, then to wear the dog collar, and later to lick the boot.

On the seventh day they lost the car. They were still about 275 miles from their goal. Marika offered to keep Driver Danesh on at a lower wage as a porter, and Danesh accepted. They continued on foot.

•

Day after day they hiked along, mile after mile, strung out in a line. Marika would stop to allow her mother to rest, and the others would pass. Then later the pair would pass the others and find themselves at the head.

Marika was at the front one day at around 5 p.m., with Trash and Oosa about fifty yards behind. The path was fairly faint, fading out completely in a clump of under-brush, but Marika saw the path appear again on the other side. Rather than go around, she went straight. Suddenly the ground gave way beneath her feet and she fell through space. Marika landed abruptly, and after a dazed moment she found she was in a pit, on a bed of spikes, fifteen feet below ground level.

Unhurt, she gasped at the sight of the deadly twelve-inch spikes. She thought herself lucky to have escaped being skewered on these cruel stakes, but then she realized that it wasn't luck, it was her dress — her cumbersome, heavy dress that held her flesh safely above the thirsty points. She laughed hard for a while, then she shouted for rescue.

Trash and Oosa came along.

"Get a vine an' pull me out," said Marika.

Trash went away. Oosa sat down on a log. The hybrid came next.

"Are you injured?"

"No," she said. "Just get a vine an' pull me out."

"A vine," he said, sitting down on the log.

Marika tugged on her earlobes as she searched for a way up the walls that were smooth, yellow, and incurved. Finally Driver Danesh appeared with Trash and a vine. They made quick work in pulling her up.

The party started off again, with Duke in the lead. Marika was ashamed of her stupid mistake for several minutes until the hybrid disappeared through the path with a yell. They hauled him out and patched his leg with green leaves.

As they finished this first-aid, Marika realized they were being watched by seven hybrids nearby. Her terror was blunted when Duke spoke to them in their alien language, saying something that made them laugh, their sharp shark teeth flashing. He conversed a bit with them and then said, "Come, they invite us to their village."

As they went to the village, Trash gave Marika a constant stream of information — that they would all be killed; that all these hybrids were female, and all hybrids were sterile like mules; that Duke would save them; that Duke would kill them himself and become the village king.

The squalid settlement was a double circle of ramshackle huts, patchwork tents, and scrap-metal shacks. Marika learned that the males were all away at a war, but would be back soon. Then the visitors went through the tedium of bartering for the rental of two rooms for the night.

Marika nodded off. Trash woke her up to lead her and Oosa to one of the shacks.

"This one is for us women," said Trash. "And the luggage. The men will be in another one."

The place was dirty, with some little bags hanging from the roof poles and insects everywhere. The hybrid women took Marika's dress with a promise to repair it for her, then Marika curled up among their suitcases and bags, fall-ing asleep in an instant.

In the middle of the night she woke up from Oosa's coughing and gagging. The air was thick with a rank odor. Marika lit a candle stub and investigated, tracing the stink to the hanging bags.

Marika handed the candle to Trash and took down the largest of the bags. To avoid losing anything of value, she emptied the bag into her Bo Peep bonnet. Out tumbled a human hand, five big toes, three eyes, and an ear. The hand was fresh, the others coated with a bluish silver slime.

"Der, dat's da one," she said, poking the hand. "Dey didn't use da gel on dat one yet."

Trash moaned and doubled over in a fight against vomiting.

"Hey, buck up," Marika told her. "Go open da door, breathe out dere."

Trash scrambled to follow these instructions while Marika scraped excessive slime off the items to spread on the hand. After Trash had gulped down some fresh air, she asked, "Purest one, how is it that you can cope with this?"

"Da gunk? From bein' a dog rancher, I guess. I done da herdin', but also da butcherin', an' dat gel is for keepin' it fresh. Dere now, see? Covered up, dat hand ain't stink no mo'. Still, Trash, dis proves you's right 'bout da danger here.

120

We gotta take turns sleepin' so's we don' get sur-prised."

After a fretful night they left the village at dawn, forgetting to retrieve the dress in their hurry.

•

Some days later Marika faced a stand off. An extended family refused to give her party food in exchange for doing farm chores, or even charity food so they would leave. At this point Marika wore a canvas sunhat, a red t-shirt advertising a brand of cigarettes that snugged jealously to her curves, and a ragged pair of pants; her arms were sunburned an angry red. They had tried playing on her biodome fame, but these stubborn Indian females seemed to know nothing of her. Driver Danesh had tried to win them over as a fellow ethnic, but had also failed. The party had run out of options, and her stomach was an empty pit of gnawing hunger. The previous farms had worked out, but now this.

She felt her frustration turn to anger. She whirled around and strode deliberately to the hybrid.

"We gotta scare deese grubbers," she muttered to him. "Take off all ya clothes, get out ya knife, an' go wif what I do."

"All right," said Duke, "but this is going to cost you a body part."

In sudden, icy fear, she asked, "Which one?" She hoped it would be a kidney, or maybe something as trivial as her appendix.

"The hair of your scalp."

She nearly laughed in relief. "Okay."

The hybrid began removing his clothes, which increased his dark menace exponentially.

"Hey," said Driver Danesh with alarm. "What is going on here?

"Quiet, all of you," said Marika. "I have to do this."

She turned to the farmwomen. "Y'all is so stingy, ya make me do dis. Look at him. He take off his clothes, he come with his knife, ya gonna wish you was never born."

Marika was pleased to see the farmers shift slightly closer together, traces of fear dawning on their faces.

"He is my devil, my curse on ya. Ya gonna wish ya done give us lots of food, half ya food, 'cause now —"

The hybrid's heavy hand dropped onto her shoulder.

"I'll take the payment now," he said.

"Now?" she squeaked, her mouth dry.

"Yes. When they see what I do to you, then they will believe."

"All right." She took off her hat, shook out her sweaty blonde curls.

"You should kneel."

Marika knelt on the hard ground, fixing the Indian women with what she hoped was a baleful glare.

Duke lifted the oily tresses off her shoulders. Her neck felt cool and refreshed as he made a quick topknot on her crown.

"No, Marika, no!" cried her mother.

"Precious one, please halt this!" cried Trash.

Marika held up her hand to them and said, "Do it now."

She gasped with surprise when the shimmering blade touched her forehead. She held her breath as it traced along her hairline down to the right, behind her ear, across the back of her neck, behind her left ear, and up to her forehead again. Then the hybrid tugged and the whole thing came off like a wig.

•

Several days later, Marika and Trash were scouting ahead in the border town of a war-torn land. They knew their party could not pass through the town since the males would be arrested or pressed into service, but the women hoped to get supplies or information.

The day was hot and lazy, and there weren't any supplies, nor any information except that the war was tentatively over. The one bright spot in the place was a fenced lot filled with hundreds of bicycles, watched over by two Chinese soldiers in a guard shack.

"Could we buy some?" murmured Marika to Trash.

"With what, purest? Besides, they can't sell them. They're soldiers, not merchants." But Trash's lips bent into a sly, knowing smile.

"So what, den?" asked Marika, trying to guess at the riddle. "We come back at night an' steal a few?"

"No, too dangerous. They might shoot."

"I give up."

"We make them give us bikes. We seduce them."

"No way."

"Easy, easy, purest — we only promise them, okay? We don't actually do anything."

"I dunno."

"Just follow my lead," said Trash, starting forward. Marika held back. Trash linked her arm in Marika's and drew her along.

The soldiers sat up with interest as the women walked toward them. Trash called out something in Chinese, and the soldiers smiled. One said something back and they waved the women over.

Marika saw that the men were young, barely twenty. The taller one said something to her, and seeing she didn't understand, he said, "English okay?"

"Yeh, English okay."

"Now the war's over, right?" said Trash. "So we should have a party, to celebrate."

The soldiers were in favor of that.

The taller one said to Marika, "Please take off your hat, for just a second."

Marika removed her hat, and they were surprised to see her bald head.

"Saturnian?" said the other one to Trash.

"No, no," said Trash, giggling coquettishly behind her scaly hand.

"I's human," said Marika, replacing the mannish sun-hat.

"We have booze and drugs hidden at another place," said Trash. "If you lend us some bikes for a little while, we will go get the stuff, come back, and party with you."

"You look kind of like Marika," said the taller one, and she saw the hungry way he looked at her.

"Who?" said Trash, her tendrils twitching.

The other soldier said, "Yeah, maybe, if she had a blonde wig."

"So lend us some bikes, and then we party," said Trash. "Okay?"

"I don't know," said the taller one, rubbing at his chin as he looked over Marika, his hunger wavering.

"Go on," said Trash to Marika. "Lift up your shirt."

"Wha —?" said Marika, feeling her heart sink. But it wasn't as bad as wearing the dog collar, or licking the boot, so she did it, briefly exposing her pale breasts tipped with pink before she turned away in shame.

The soldiers lent them two bicycles and never saw them again.

•

Five people and two bicycles. The males pedaled and the women rode.

The detour around the border town was long. Oosa's health was failing. They found a doctor, but he demanded payment upfront.

Marika felt a panic. She shifted her mother over to Trash and stepped off the wide porch, past Driver Danesh, to stand before Duke.

"I need some money ta fix up my mamma."

"Every body comes to an end," said the hybrid. "Maybe it is time to let her go."

"No! She's all I got left. I got to sell you something. Tell me what."

"Well, you know, there are rules . . ." Duke stroked his

chin, thinking on it. "For you, it should be something that doesn't show. I guess that means it could be a kidney or a lung, but you still need those, so it should be something that is not so necessary to daily life."

"Like a little toe?"

"Yes, but that isn't worth enough. I know! A little lump of flesh, like the tip of your ear lobe, only no one will see it."

•

Marika sold that little button of meat and gave the money to the doctor, who began treating Oosa.

Oosa died despite all the efforts. Through her terrible black sorrow, Marika was desperate to raise enough money to cremate her body to keep it from the aliens. Again she turned to the hybrid.

"Duke, I gotta sell something. Please!"

"Luck has been bad for you. Maybe you should just quit. Make a life for yourself here."

"But den everythin' we done is fer nuthin'. Dere ain't nuthin' here, you know dat — da boom town is at Sky Train. Please, ain't dere sumpin' else I can sell? Kidney? Lung?"

"No, no," said Duke. "Now it will be something that shows. What fills up your shirt."

•

After the cremation, the four of them went on. Marika was now bald and flat-chested, a genderless person, looking like a boy with wide hips and swollen thighs. Driver Danesh was better than when he had started, owing to the fact that at every opportunity during the trip he had upgraded his cyborg parts. In a similar way, Trash had improved herself by spending her money on mutagenic alien foods and substances — her ears had fallen off and all her skin was now pebbled, so that she hardly seemed human any longer. Duke was the only one who seemed unchanged.

They began scrounging food from garbage bins. Trash wept silently the first time Marika ate alien food scraps, risking mutation, and she no longer called her "purest" after that.

There were days when they smoked cigarette butts for energy and hunger suppression, nights when they slept on the roadside in utter exhaustion.

At last they came to Station City, out on the Serengeti Plain.

The city was a lot like Liboweier, in being full of aliens and having a mixture of buildings active and abandoned. Marika was doubtful, then disappointed.

"But where's da mountain?" she cried. "An' how come I ain't been hearin' da boom — should be one every hour!"

"The boom is heard on the east side of the mountain," said Driver Danesh, "not on the west side. And the mountain is seventy-five miles away."

"Seventy-five?! Another seventy-five miles?"

"The space cars cover it in seconds. Somehow or another the space cars are loaded into the underground tube here, and fired like a bullet that comes out at the mountain top, way over there."

The guards at the gate would not allow Marika to enter without a sponsor from inside or the posting of a bond. She gave the name of Uncle Sugar, but they checked and said he was not there. She tried Johnny Jingo, Legal Eagle, and even Jimmy Gimme. It did not work. The guards said that none of her relatives were there.

Another barrier, here at this penultimate stage, was still a bad surprise for Marika. In a sense she had been toughened by her travel, giving her a rhino hide, but in another sense her layers had been removed, leaving her the skin of a tomato, such that this new barrier cut right through her, straight to her heart, which erupted with rage and defiance. At the eye of the storm she knew that she had only herself, that there was no other help, that there was no other way.

She took a deep breath, let it out. She knew what to do, and she promised herself it would be the last time.

"Duke," she said, "before ya go in, come over here a ways. I wanna talk wif you."

"Listen," he said. "You and the others can make some money here, outside the wall. Maybe not enough to get in, but —"

"Take one o' my ovaries."

His mouth snapped shut. He looked at her in silence, then said, "The law is very plain about that."

"Which mean dat da price is bestest."

Duke's eyes bulged out. Sweat beaded on his brow. The tables seemed to have turned. Silently he walked into a maze of empty buildings, and after telling the others to wait, she followed.

The buildings seemed to be mainly temporary structures from when the space cannon was being built: dorms, beer halls, laundries, gambling dens, warehouses, and the like. Deep inside the maze, Duke led Marika into a dingy surgical suite lit by a dim naked bulb. He stood facing a corner. She took off her clothes, her shoes, her pants, her shirt, and her panties. She choked back a moan at the sight of her flattened chest, sudden tears spilling from her eyes, then she climbed up on the surgery bed.

"I is ready," she said.

Duke turned around slowly, stiffly. He advanced haltingly, step by step, with heavy breathing and his wide eyes darting around a circuit of her hips, her thighs, her loins. She closed her eyes, but she could feel his gaze, like laser beams, spiraling in from hips, to thighs, to loins, over and over again.

"Woman, you tempt me too far!" he roared. She opened her eyes in time to see Duke drive a spike through her head. As her sight grew dim, he blurred. Hoisting her up, he pushed her against the wall and drove the spike into the wall so that she dangled there like a pinned butterfly.

Then the blur was gone and she was alone. The light

stopped fading. Marika hung there, thinking of the steps that brought her to this fate, over and over again, and the hours turned into days. She remembered the time when she had lost the dress, and in the room the dust fell upon her like the hot ash from a spewing volcano. She recalled how she had sold her scalp, believing it was just her hair, and on the wall the days turned into years. Again she sold her clitoris, then her breasts, but then her mind jumped back to when she was back on the road. While posing nude, the line they had her say was, "Twenty-five in one night," which she repeated so many times that it went through all shades of meaning and became meaningless. While wearing the dog collar, her line was "My Plot of Three Daggers," which never meant anything to her, nor did her boot-licking line, "I rejected the Hundred Days' Reform," and yet even though the words meant nothing, still cool tears of shame had skipped lightly down her burning cheeks to patter against the floorboards, while in the medical suite around her the years turned into decades.

Suddenly there was a blurry motion, then there were two. A blur came close, very close, and all at once Marika fell, as if gravity had returned, but her body was softly stopped by a blur.

Marika's vision cleared, the room grew brighter, and she was surprised to see Trash and Driver Danesh. Both seemed untouched by the passing of decades. They were talking to Marika, but she could not understand. It was something about a city, a duke who did wrong, and going home.

She was so happy to see them her heart was ham-mering in her chest and tears were streaming down her face. They were trying so hard to help her, and she said yes, yes. She marveled at the years, the decades, and they clouded up, saying it had only been days, weeks. Then she cried in pain and confusion, but they comforted her, saying it was all right now.

They took Marika to a Saturnian surgeon who reinstall-ed her parts. They took her to a Gray tailor who gave her a new Marie Antoinette Bo-Peep uniform that was even better than her old one. They took her back home by mag-lev train to Liboweier, the place of her birth, where the city put her in a mansion, cherishing her as the last American.

After all this flurry of activity, she found herself alone for an hour. It was a relief. From her balcony she looked out over the city in the long late afternoon. She spotted the ruins of the biodome. She tried to find meaning in what she had gone through, but all she could come up with was, *I was stripped down to nuthin'. No, first I was called bad names, every bad name, an' run out like a animal, some dirty animal. I was pollution. Den I was stripped down to nuthin', an' I was nuthin'. Later on I was builded up, an' bringed back, but I is no more da same as before.*

Beneath it all she felt the itching fear that the whole thing would happen again. She recognized that possibility, and vowed that she would do things differently the next time

MICHAEL ANDRE-DRIUSSI

NOTES ON THE STORIES

"White Japan" was published in a fiction anthology on the University of California, Berkeley campus. At that point I had visited Japan, but not yet lived there.

"The Ragnarockenroll Overture" was published in a small press anthology (*Air Fish*) and a magazine (*The Silver Web*). Beatlemania.

"Mad Dogs Raid Mars" is a sequel to "Mad Dogs of Mercury," a space adventure collected in *Old Flames Burn Manvi*. This one is an idea from my teenage years, a response to the Iranian Hostage Crisis with a sort of *Star-ship Troopers* action.

"The Slushpile Surfer" is about the future of telecommuting, which was a hot topic at the time.

"Doomsday Tours" was a cover story for Algis Budrys's magazine. I took the background of a new caliphate and a rising China from an article in *The Economist* I had read while living in Japan for a couple years. I wanted the story to be a '70s kind of thing, like a John Brunner piece.

"Tex of the Dobermans" was published in my old magazine.

"Aliens with Candy" is a nightmare and a myth.

"Mentally Gifted Mutants" appeared in an obscure Australian magazine about superheroes.

"It's a Long Road to the Sky Train" is set in the same universe as "Aliens with Candy." It owes a lot to explorer Mary Kingsley, as well as tales of young women recounted in *Savage Continent: Europe in the Aftermath of World War II*.

MICHAEL ANDRE-DRIUSSI

ABOUT THE AUTHOR

Michael Andre-Driussi, mainly known for his World Fantasy Award-nominated science fiction reference book *Lexicon Urthus,* has achieved some notice regarding thirty-four stories published in such venues as *Bastion, Black Denim Lit,* and *Big Pulp.* Many of these fictions have been collected in *Fallout Stories* (2016), *The Jizmatic Trilogy* (2017), and *Old Flames Burn Manvi* (forthcoming).